SMIDGEN PRESS

Happily Owned By:

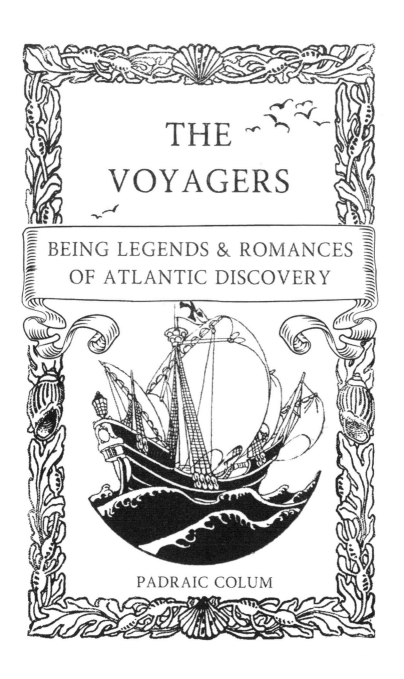

THE VOYAGERS

BEING LEGENDS & ROMANCES OF ATLANTIC DISCOVERY

PADRAIC COLUM

THE VOYAGERS

Edition copyright © 2022 by Smidgen Press
Contains unabridged public domain material by Padraic Colum.
Illustrations by Wilfred Jones.

Originally published in 1925 by The Macmillan Company and printed by J. J. Little and Ives Company, NY. The body of this public domain work is unedited, unrevised material and, as such, may contain outdated ideas and terminology. Smidgen Press and its employees and contractors are not responsible for any views expressed in this book.

Cover by Terri Shown
Introduction by JacQueline V. Roe
Typeset by Skinner Book Services
Set in Garamond Premiere Pro

ISBN: 978-1-950536-29-0 (paperback)
      978-1-950536-30-6 (hardcover)
      978-1-950536-31-3 (dust jacket)

Pocket hardcover available at SmidgenPress.com

To Vilhjalmur Stefansson
Great Voyager
Great Adventurer

PADRAIC COLUM

Playwright, poet, and novelist Padraic Colum, born "Patrick Columb," began his life in Ireland. His father was the master of the Longford Union Workhouse, a facility where the poor were granted work and lodging—and it is here that young Patrick is believed to have picked up a love of stories as he grew to know the inmates.

When his father lost his job, Patrick moved to be with his mother's people. With his uncle, he traveled to fairs, meeting storytellers and ballad singers. All this laid further groundwork for the great literary figure he would become.

The family reunited in Dublin, but once again his father lost his job. This time, Patrick was old enough to help. Foregoing further formal education, at age seventeen he passed an exam and became a clerk—but it would not stop him from becoming the writer he was destined to be.

His early published poems caught the notice of

literary greats like poet W.B. Yeats, publicist George William Russell, and Irish dramatist and folklorist Augusta, Lady Gregory. Now known as Padraic Colum, he became an integral member of the talent in the Irish Literary Revival, many of whose members were tied to the founding of the Abbey Theatre (later the National Theatre of Ireland). In later times, his realistic plays have been credited with being foundational in developing modern Irish theatre. At the time, though, he was only able to pursue writing full-time due to a generous five-year scholarship provided by American benefactor Thomas Hughes Kelly.

It was not until after marrying writer and literary critic Mary Maguire that doors opened for him as a writer. The couple visited the United States in 1914, planning a visit for a few short months. While in America, they discovered Padraic could actually make a living as a writer, and they decided to remain in the United States. At this point, he began writing for children, receiving Newbery Honor medals for three of his books: *The Golden Fleece and the Heroes Who Lived before Achilles* (awarded 1922); *The Voyagers: Being Legends and Romances* * of Atlantic Discovery* (1926);

---

* The official subtitle on the book's title page was "Being Legends and *Romances*," but whether due to a last-minute change or a miscommunication, the subtitle printed on the cover was "Being Legends and *Histories*."

and *Big Tree of Bunlahy: Stories of My Own Country-side* (1934).

His acclaim led the Hawaiian legislature to hire him to take their folklore and make them into children's stories that would be later used as curriculum. After extensive research, including learning some of the language and interviewing locals, he wrote three volumes of stories. These books are held in such high regard that when then-President Barack Obama visited Ireland, he was presented with the books*, a nod to both his Hawaiian and Irish heritage.

In the early 1930s, Colum and his wife returned to Europe and worked with James Joyce. Later, they went on to write a memoir entitled *Our Friend James Joyce*, which Colum completed after Mary passed away.

At the time of Colum's death, he had published over sixty books and is still celebrated at an annual festival held in Longford, Ireland, the land of his birth.

---

* EPIC The Irish Emigration Museum in Dublin. n.d. "Padraic Colum, who preserved the local lore of Longford – and Hawaii." https://epicchq.com/story/padraic-colum-the-irishman-who-preserved-the-local-lore-of-longford-and-hawaii/ [Accessed 15 April 2022].

CONTENTS

Publisher's note: Since this book's release in 1925, our culture has moved, appropriately, toward recognizing the need for multiple viewpoints when considering exploration and colonization practices.

In *The Voyagers*, Colum writes about Jamestown, Virginia (with Chief Powhatan and Pocahontas); Christopher Columbus; and Ponce de Leon, among others. In addition to Colum's own research notes at the end of the book, we have added some books we believe contain helpful modern perspectives under "Suggested Reading" on p. 203.

THE TOWER ABOVE THE OCEAN

Often, upon a path that went along the coast, there walked a swarthy, strong-featured man wearing a round barret cap on his head and wrapped in a large mantle. This man was all in black except for the gilt spurs that were at his heels. Those who met him made reverence to him, for he was Prince Henry, the son of the great King of Portugal.

They would often see him halt in his walk, and stand and remain standing long, with his hand to his brow, looking over the main ocean. Out there, the people thought, were the wind-demons that the Arabs told them of; out there was that sea with snaky sea-weed

1

That swarthy man would stand there looking across the sea . . .

that their ships had once come to and had not been able to sail through—the sea that, according to what wise men said, was over the lost land of Atlantis. And when they saw Prince Henry looking out over the ocean, they became fearful, thinking that he was about to order ships to sail out there.

Below where he walked there was a shipyard and a harbor. In one, ships were built for him, and from the other they sailed, each ship with a great cross upon its sail. They sailed towards the south, not out into the main ocean, not towards the west. And above where he walked was a high tower that he had built.

The tower was built in a lonely place, upon a cliff that went down steeply into the ocean. To the people of the country it seemed to be the tower of a magician. From the top of the tower wise men whom Prince Henry had caused to come to him watched and studied the courses of the stars.

Prince Henry, named the Navigator, the son of the King of Portugal, dreamed of a land beyond the ocean, and of ways to come to that land. He had the tower built there so that he might constantly watch across the ocean from it, and that wise men might study from the top of it the courses by which ships might sail into the west. In the tower were maps engraved upon a metal and charts painted upon parchments. And men who had traveled far, or who knew the histories of those who had traveled far, were brought by the prince to his tower above the Atlantic Ocean in the hope that they would help him towards that which he sought—certain knowledge of a land beyond and of ways to come to it.

To the west, but not far to the west, the captains of the prince's ships discovered islands that they named Porto Santo and Madeira. But farther west they would not sail, for they were daunted by that empty space and their ignorance of what lay beyond what they sighted. The prince considered that what lay beyond was land, a larger land than that to which his ships had come. And, that his captains might be put into spirit for making quest of it, he had sent for and he had brought to his tower men who had heard whatever rumors there were concerning that land.

Men came to Prince Henry who knew of that land from legends and histories of former times: from all parts of Europe they came; some from the east, and some from the north. They stayed with him in his castle. After they had been with him for a while he took them into his tower, and he gave a banquet to them and to the captains who had sailed his ships.

Amongst those who came there was a tall man with a flowing beard who looked grave as though bearing much knowledge. He was a Greek, and was from the great city of Constantinople. When the banquet was ended the prince called upon him to speak to the captains and to the learned men who were there. Then that grave man rose up; he went and stood upon the platform that was the prow of an ancient ship, a rostrum. He saluted the prince, and speaking to him and to the captains and the other learned men who were there, he said:

"O prince and ye captains, and learned men who have come from afar! What I am going to relate to you is an ancient history, a history that is known only to those who can read our language and who have our ancient books." He stood upon the ship's prow facing them all; the tower was lighted up; the maps and charts and spheres that the prince had brought there were all around. The learned Greek looked upon Prince Henry and his captains, and on the learned men, his companions (each of whom would have to tell about the land to the west), and he related:

THE LEGEND OF ATLANTIS

Plato, our great philosopher, told what I shall tell to you now. It came to Plato from Solon, his ancestor; it was handed down from Solon's time, a tradition that came from father to son for many generations. First it was told by a priest of Egypt to Solon, the wise man of Greece. Solon thought of making a poem about it, but he had much to do after he had returned from Egypt, and he was never able to do more than make a beginning for the poem.

In days that are thousands of years away, the Egyptian priest told Solon, there was a great island in front of the straits that are between the Columns of Heracles,

There was a great and wonderful empire.

as the Greeks called them. That island, situated in the Atlantic Ocean, was very large—it was larger than Libya and Asia Minor together, and it was on the way to islands farther west in the ocean. From those farther islands people could pass to a continent that was opposite.

In the island that lay opposite the Columns of Heracles there was a great and wonderful empire, an empire which had rule over the several islands as well as over parts of the continent—our continent—to the east of it. But first of all (these are the words of the Egyptian priest to Solon) I shall have to tell you of the origin of those who were the people of the great island that was called Atlantis, and of the islands beyond.

In the center of the great island there was a plain which is said to have been the fairest of the world's plains, and the most fertile. Near the plain, and also in the center of the island, was a mountain which was not very high on any side. On this mountain dwelt a man of the primeval race, a man whose name was Evenor; he had an only daughter whose name was Cleito. Now Poseidon, the god of the sea, saw and loved Cleito. He broke the ground and enclosed the hill on which she dwelt, making all round the hill alternate zones, land and then water, water and then land, the zones encircling one another. In the center he made two springs to come up, one of warm water and the other of cold, and he made every variety of foodplants to grow abundantly upon the plain.

Poseidon, married to Cleito, had ten children, all male; he divided the great island into ten portions; to his first-born son he gave his mother's dwelling and the surrounding allotment, and he made him king over the rest; the nine other sons he made princes, and he gave them rule over men and territory. The eldest son was named Atlas, and from him the island received the name "Atlantis," and the whole ocean was named "Atlantic."

Atlas had many children, and the kingship of the island was handed down by him to his eldest son, who handed it down to his eldest son, and so on for many generations. Never was there so wealthy a reigning family as were the kings of Atlantis. Their lands were most fertile; there was upon the island abundance of wood for carpentry and shipbuilding; there were animals wild and tame, amongst them elephants in great numbers. Also, whatever fragrant growths there are in the earth, whether roots, or herbage, or fragrant wood, or flowers that might be distilled, grew and thrived in that land, as well as fruits of every kind. Indeed, that sacred island lying beneath the sun brought forth all things that were fair and wondrous in infinite abundance.

Moreover, there were rich minerals in the earth; there

men dug up that metal which is now only a name, but which was then something more than a name—orichalcum; with the exception of gold this was deemed the most precious of metals amongst the people of those days.

The men of the island employed themselves in constructing temples and palaces and harbors and docks. They bridged over the zones of water which surrounded the ancient metropolis, and they made a passage into and out of the royal palace. That palace they continued to ornament in successive generations, every king surpassing the one who went before him to the utmost of his power, until the building was made a marvel for spaciousness and for beauty. The island on which the palace was situated they surrounded by a stone wall, on either side placing towers and gates and bridges where the sea passed in. The stone that was needed for this work they quarried from underneath the center island, and from underneath the zones, on the outer as well as on the inner side. One kind of stone was white, another black, and a third, red. Some of their buildings were simple, but in others they put together different stones, which they intermingled for the sake of ornament, and to be a natural source of delight. The entire circuit of the wall which was outermost was covered with brass, the circuit of the next wall was coated with tin, and the third, which encompassed the citadel, flashed with the red gleam of orichalcum.

The palace in the interior of the citadel was constructed in this way: in the center was a temple dedicated to Cleito and Poseidon, the founders of the kingly race, which was surrounded by an enclosure of gold; this was the spot in which the race of Atlas and his brothers were born. Thither the people annually brought the fruits of the earth in their season and made sacrifices. Here was Poseidon's own temple. It had a sort of barbaric splendour; all outside the temple, with the exception of the pinnacles, was covered with silver; the pinnacles were covered with gold. In the interior of the temples the roof was of ivory adorned everywhere with gold and silver and orichalcum; all the other parts of the walls and pillars and floor were lined with orichalcum.

In the temple they placed statues of gold; there was Poseidon standing on his chariot, the driver of six-winged horses; the statue was of such size that it touched the roof. Around Poseidon were a hundred Nereids riding on dolphins. Outside the temple there were statues of gold representing the first ten kings of the island, and their wives.

There were gardens and places for exercise. In the center of the larger island there was a race-course that extended all round the island; horses raced in it. The docks were full of galleys and naval stores. The city beside its harbor was crowded with habitations, and the harbor was filled with vessels of merchants coming from all parts.

The country was very lofty and precipitous on the side of the sea; but about the city and surrounding it there was a level plain, itself enclosed by mountains which descended towards the sea. This plain was smooth and even. The whole region of the island lay towards the south, and it was sheltered from the north. The mountains surrounding the plain in their height and in their form surpassed all mountains that are now anywhere to be seen.

The plain had been cultivated during many ages by many generations of kings. It was enclosed by a trench that went round it in a circle: the depth and width and length of this trench were incredible; they gave the impression that such work could hardly be wrought by the hand of man. The trench was excavated to the depth of a hundred feet, and its breadth was a stadium everywhere. It was carried round the whole extent of the plain, and its length was ten thousand stadia. This trench received the streams that came down from the mountains; they were brought here and there across the plain and made to touch upon the city at various points; through the trench they were let off into the sea.

From above, straight canals of a hundred feet in width were cut in the plain, and let off into the trench towards the sea; by them wood was brought down from the mountains to the city and the fruits of the mountain farms were brought down to the ships.

The laws that governed Atlantis and the dependent islands had been inscribed by the first men on a column of orichalcum which was set up at the temple of Poseidon in the middle of the island. There the people assembled every fifth and sixth year alternately. And when they were gathered together they consulted about public affairs, and inquired if anyone had transgressed in anything, and passed judgment upon him accordingly. But before passing judgment they gave pledges to one another in this wise:

There were bulls that had the range of the temple of Poseidon; the ten princes who were left alone in the temple, after they had offered prayers to the gods, hunted the bulls, without weapons, but with staves and nooses. When they had taken the bull they led him up to the column that the laws were inscribed upon; they then struck him on the head, and slew him over the sacred inscription. Now, on the column, beside the laws, there was inscribed an oath invoking mighty curses on the disobedient. After offering sacrifice according to their customs, the princes mingled a cup and cast a clot of blood for each of them. They then drew from the golden vessels a portion for each, and pouring a libation on the fire they swore that they would judge according to the laws inscribed on the column, and that they would punish anyone who had previously transgressed, and that, for the future, they would not transgress any of the laws inscribed, and would not obey any ruler who commanded them to act otherwise than according to the laws left them by Poseidon. The most important of the laws were that they, the princes, were not to take up arms against one another, and that they were all to come to the rescue if anyone in the city attempted to overthrow the royal house. They were to deliberate in common about war and other matters, giving the supremacy to the family of Atlas. The king was not to have the power of life and death over any of his kinsmen unless he had the assent of the majority of the princes.

And when darkness had come on, and the fire on the sacrificial altar was low, all the princes put on the most beautiful azure robes, and, sitting on the ground, drew near the embers of the sacrifice, and, extinguishing all the fires about the temple, they received and gave judgment. And when they had given judgment, at daybreak, they wrote down their sentences on golden tablets, and deposited them as memorials in the temple with their robes.

For many generations, as long as the divine nature lasted in them, the people of Atlantis were obedient to the laws, and well disposed towards the gods, for they possessed true and, in every way, great spirits; they practised gentleness and wisdom in their intercourse with one another; they thought lightly of all the great possessions they had: wealth did not deprive them of self-control; they were not intoxicated by luxury; they were temperate and they were able to see clearly.

And by this clear sight, and by the continuance in them of the divine nature, their power and possessions grew and increased. But something happened to the people of Atlantis—the divine portion in them began to fade away. It became diluted too often and too much with the mortal admixture; human nature got the upper hand. Then they, being unable to bear their great fortune, became insolent and adopted unseemly ways; to him who had eyes to see they began to appear bare, as having lost their fairest and most precious gifts. To themselves they still appeared glorious and blessed, and that at the very time they were filled with unrighteous power.

Then Zeus, the god of gods, who rules with law and who is able to see into such things, perceiving that a race once honorable was in a most wretched decline, collected all the gods into his habitation, which, being placed in the center of the world, permits him to see all things that are mortal. And when he had called them all together, Zeus spoke to the gods . . .

So Plato foreshadowed but did not tell what happened there. We do not know and there is no tradition concerning the fate of Atlantis and its people. It may be that Zeus destroyed the land by great floods such as are spoken of in one of our legends; it may be that he destroyed it by earthquakes and fires such as are spoken of in a tale that the Arabs tell of a city of theirs that was destroyed in ancient times; it may be that Atlantis was destroyed by earthquakes and fires and floods. We know that there is no longer a great island in the ocean opposite the Columns of Heracles; that is, opposite the extremity of your kingdom, prince. But in the legend that Plato has handed down, islands other than the great island named Atlantis are spoken of, and a continent beyond them. It may be that some of these islands survived whatever catastrophe came upon great Atlantis; it may be that they can still be reached, and that they stretch out like stepping-stones to that continent that is spoken of in the ancient tradition—the continent that touches upon the real ocean.

He made an end, and the learned men and captains who were at the tables spoke together, saying how wonderful it would be to come upon islands in the middle of the ocean that were parts of the empire of Atlantis. And one spoke of Antilia, the Island of the Seven Cities, that was said to be far out in the ocean. And others spoke fearfully, telling of a Sea of Darkness that Arabian sailors had been blown into—Arabian sailors who had once sailed out of Lisbon. Then, after a while, Prince Henry called upon another of the learned men who were there. The one called upon rose up and went and stood on the rostrum.

He was a bearded man, with a short nose and merry eyes, and he looked like one who might have a sword beneath his scholar's cloak. He saluted Prince Henry, and to him and to the captains and learned men who were there he told:

THE VOYAGE OF MAELDUIN

There was a famous man in Ireland, Ailill by
name, who had a son who was called Maelduin.
The boy never knew his father. When he was
an infant he was taken from his mother by the queen
of the land, and he was reared up with the children of
the king and queen. He grew up to be a very handsome
youth, and he was full of brightness and playfulness
and gayety. When he was a young warrior he outdid
all his comrades in throwing the ball, in running and
in leaping, in racing horses and in pitching the stone.

One day, after he had pitched the stone very far,
thereby defeating a proud young warrior who was

pitching against him, this young warrior said to him and to those who were around him, "So we are defeated by Maelduin who does not know who his father and his mother are, nor from what race he has sprung." When Maelduin heard this said it was as if a spear had gone through him. He went away from that place, and he went to where his foster-mother, the queen, was, and he asked her if she were not his mother, and if the king were not his father. The queen did not give an answer to him, and then Maelduin said, "I will not take food nor drink till thou tell me who my father and my mother are." Then the queen said, "I am thy mother, for none ever loved her son more than I love thee." Maelduin was not content with that answer, and he pleaded with the queen to tell him what his birth was. Thereafter the queen took him to see his own mother who was her friend.

His mother told him that his father was Ailill of the island of Arran. Then to Arran across the strip of sea, Maelduin went, and his foster-brothers, the queen's three sons, of their own accord went with him. And in Arran he was kindly received by his father's kindred. But his father was not now living.

In Arran Maelduin became the leader of the youths in all the sports of youth. One day he was pitching the stone; where he was pitching it was within the walls of a church that had been burned and destroyed. As he had the stone raised in his hands, his feet were set upon the blackened flagstone that was on the floor of the church. It was then that a monk who was standing by the wall of the church said to him, "It would be fitter for thee to go forth and avenge the man who lies under this stone than to be casting thy stone over his blackened bones." "What man lies here?" asked Maelduin. "Ailill, thy father," said the monk. "Who slew him?" asked Maelduin. "Reivers from Leix," said the monk. "They burned the church and they slew thy father upon this spot."

Then Maelduin dropped the stone that he was about to pitch, and he put his mantle about him, and he went to his home. He told his relatives that he would go to Leix and find out the man who had killed his father and avenge his death upon him. But they told him that there was no ship that he could sail in from Arran.

Maelduin went to a wizard, and the wizard gave him directions for the making of a boat; he told Maelduin, too, when he should sail and how many companions he should take on his voyage—he was to take seventeen, and no more than seventeen were to be allowed to go with him into the boat.

He and his friends worked on the boat, and they finished it and made it ready for sea. Then Maelduin gathered his seventeen companions, and hoisted his sail and pushed out of the harbor.

Just then his three foster-brothers came down on the beach. They implored him to take them with him. "Get you home," cried Maelduin, "for none but the number I have with me may sail upon this voyage." His foster-brothers would not listen to him; they threw themselves into the water and they swam out towards the boat. Then Maelduin had to turn the boat back; to save them from being drowned he picked them up and took them into the boat. Then they sailed off to find the man who had slain his father before Maelduin was born.

For a day and for half of the next night they sailed on. They came then to two small and bare islands on which there were fortresses. As they drew near they heard the noise of armed men quarreling in one of the fortresses. "Stand off from me," one voice cried, "for I am a better man than thou. 'Twas I who slew Ailill of Arran in the church of Doocloone and burned the church over him, and none of his kinsmen has ever dared to try and avenge his death upon me. And thou hast done nothing to equal that."

And when they in the boat heard these words they cried out that God had guided them to this place, and they called upon Maelduin to make ready to take vengeance upon the slayer of his father. But even as they spoke a great wind came up, and it drove their boat away from the islands and out into the boundless ocean. Then Maelduin said to his three foster-brothers, "You are to blame that our voyage did not have an end at this place, and even now I had avenged the death of my father, for you three came on board in spite of the words of the wizard to me." The three foster-brothers made no answer to this.

The First Islands in the Boundless Ocean

Then for three days and three nights the boat drifted out and into the ocean; then they came to an island that had great trees all around it. Great birds were resting in the branches of these great trees. Maelduin and his companions landed on that island, and they were able to kill some of the birds; some of those they killed they ate on the island, and some they brought to provision the boat.

They sailed on again and then they came to an island that had a sandy beach. There was a strange beast upon that island. Its body was like a horse's body, but instead of hoofs it had claws. It raced over the beach towards the mariners; they pushed off the boat and they got clear away. But the beast was able to take up great pebbles in its claws; it cast them at the boat as they rowed away.

And after that they came to an island that was flat

and grassy. Two of the mariners were sent to explore it. They went upon it, but they saw no sign of life on the island. But going farther on they came upon a vast green race-course, and upon the course there were marks of horses' hoofs, each hoofmark as big as the sail of a ship. The two were frightened, and they came running back to their companions on the beach. And when they told them of the monstrous marks they had seen the mariners went into their boat and they pushed out to sea.

And then from the sea they saw a horse-race upon the island; they heard the shouting of a great multitude as they cheered on the horses, the white horse and the brown horse. They saw horses of a giant size, and they were racing more swiftly than the wind. Maelduin and his companions rowed away with all their might, for they were made fearful by what they saw.

They sailed on for a week, and then they came to a high island that had a house standing on the shore. The house had a door of stone opening into the sea, and through the door the sea kept hurling salmon into the house. Maelduin and his companions went within; the house was empty of folk, but there was a great bed within it, and the bed was all made ready for the chief that the house belonged to; there were smaller beds for the chief's attendants, and meat and drink were beside each bed. Maelduin and his companions ate and drank

their fill there, sitting upon the beds, and then they went
back to their boat and they sailed out on the sea again.

The Precipitous Island, the Island of the Strange Beast, and the Island of the Fiery Swine

Thereafter they were a long time upon the open sea without coming to any island. The food and drink they had
taken with them gave out, and they were now hungry
and thirsty. They sailed on, all in very great hardship.
At last they came in sight of an island. But it was an
island with high, precipitous sides, and the mariners
could make no landing on it. Trees hung down from
the precipices that were the sides of the island; as the
boat passed along, Maelduin broke off a twig from one
of the trees, and he kept it in his hand. They went without finding any inlet or landing-place upon it. But now
upon the twig that Maelduin held a cluster of apples
grew. He shared them with his companions. And these
apples sufficed to take hunger and thirst away from each
of the mariners. They sailed twice around it, and then,
putting off from that island, they went out to sea again.

After sailing for many days they came to an island
that had a fence all round it—a fence of stone. Inside the
fence they saw a huge and most curious beast. It raced
around and around within the fence, and then it raced
up the hill that topped the island; there, in sight of all

the mariners, it performed a marvelous feat; that beast turned its body within its skin, round and round, the skin remaining unmoved while it did this; and then it turned its skin round and round on its body, the body remaining unmoved while it did this. After that the strange beast raced down the hill to get at the mariners. It could not get at them across the fence of stone. But as Maelduin and his companions rowed away it took up stones and it pelted them. One of the stones went through Maelduin's shield, and lodged in the keel of the boat. As for the beast, it galloped up the hill again as the mariners drew off, and there it turned its skin round and round on its unmoving body

They sailed on, but now the mariners had become down-cast and disheartened; they were weary of the long voyage, and they felt that the way home was lost to them. Soon, however, they came to another island. They saw trees upon it that were loaded with fruits that were like bright-hued apples. But they also saw under the trees beasts that were like swine, but were red and fiery. These beasts kicked at the trees; the apples fell and the beasts devoured them. There were birds on the island, too. When the beasts came under the trees the birds swam out into the sea, and they remained upon the sea until evening, when they turned and swam back again, the beasts now being gone.

Maelduin and his companions, watching the island, saw that the swine-like beasts came under the trees only in the morning. The mariners waited until night-fall, and then they landed on the island, and they went amongst the trees, gathering the bright-hued apples. As they went they felt the ground hot under them from the fiery swine in their caverns below. They gathered the fruit which was good against both hung and thirst; they loaded their boat with what they gathered, and they sailed away greatly refreshed.

The Island of the Little Cat

Then they came to the Island of the Little Cat. That island was like a white tower of chalk rising up to the sky almost, with a rampart on the top around houses that were as white as snow. They landed on that island and they climbed up to the rampart; then they went into the largest of the white houses. There were no folk in that house; the only living creature there was a little cat; it went leaping from one another of the four pillars that were set up in the midst of the house. The little cat looked on the mariners, but it did not cease from play, but still went leaping from one pillar to the other. On the walls of that house were rows of precious things—a row of gold and silver brooches, a row of torques or gold-twisted collars, a row of swords with golden and silver hilts. Quilts and shining garments lay on the floor of the house.

And there was also a roasted ox, and a boiled flitch of bacon, and a cauldron of liquor. When the mariners looked on these viands they longed to eat, for they had had no meat since they had eaten the birds they killed on one of the first islands they had come to. Maelduin, looking at the little cat, said, "Hath this been left for us?" The cat ceased from play and looked at them for a moment, and then went on playing again. Maelduin took this for an assent, so he gave permission to the mariners to eat and drink there, and rest themselves in the house. They feasted there, and then they slept. They took what remained of the food and liquor, and they brought it to their vessel and stored it there.

As they were leaving the house the youngest of Maelduin's foster-brothers, who had been looking on the precious things in rows on the wall, took down a twisted collar of gold. Now this was against the command that Maelduin had given to all the mariners. As soon as the youth had taken it off its peg, the little cat leaped at him; it went through him like a fiery arrow, and the youngest of Maelduin's foster-brothers fell down in ashes on the floor. The little cat stood on a pillar looking angrily on the men. Then Maelduin took up the collar of twisted gold and put it back on its peg on the wall, and soothed the cat, until it went on with its play again, leaping from pillar to pillar. The mariners took the ashes of the dead youth and they strewed them upon the seashore, and they went back to their vessel, and put out to sea again. It was thus that one of the youths who had gone with Maelduin against the word of the wizard lost his life. And so the mariners came to and went from the Island of the Little Cat.

The Island with the Bridge of Glass

From the Island of the Little Cat they sailed on until they came to an island that was the most wonderful of all the islands they had yet seen. On this island there was a fortress with a brazen door to it, and with a bridge of glass that led up to it. The mariners, when they landed, were for going up to the fortress. But when they put their feet upon the bridge of glass it threw them off backwards. Do what they would they could not cross that shining bridge; every time one stood upon it it threw him off. They stood there looking across it and at the brazen door beyond it. Through that door they saw a woman come. She had a pail in her hand, and she lifted up one of the glass slats of the bridge, and she let her pail down and into the water beneath; she lifted it up and went with her pail into the fortress.

The mariners then struck the brazen ends of the

The bridge of glass threw them off backwards.

bridge to announce their coming and to demand admittance into the fortress. But the sound given out by the stricken metal was so melodious that it lulled all of them to sleep. They slept until the next morning, and as they wakened up they saw the woman come out of the fortress again, and they saw her lower her pail and draw it up again out of the water. And looking at the mariners the woman said, "Are we so secure that these great voyagers cannot come to us?" After she had gone within they struck the brazen ends of the bridge again, and again the melody that came from the stricken metal lulled them to sleep. They slumbered until morning when they saw the woman come out from the brazen door again with her pail and lower it into the water below; again she spoke to them, mocking them, and went into the fortress with her pail.

On the fourth day the woman came through the brazen door and came to them over the bridge of glass. She was beautiful, with hair of bright gold, with a circlet of gold upon her head, and with a white mantle around her; on her feet were silver sandals, and next her body was a smooth silken smock.

"Welcome to thee, O Maelduin," said the woman, and then she welcomed the mariners, each by his own name. She brought them across the bridge and within the fortress, and she gave them couches to rest on, and food and drink to refresh themselves with. All the food and drink came out of the pail that she carried. And the mariners eating that food and drinking that liquor found each the taste that he liked best on it.

When she left them the mariners spoke to each other and said: "Why should not Maelduin marry this fair woman, and why should we not stay resting here after our long voyage? It is plain now that we shall never find our way back to our own land." And when he heard this from them, Maelduin said, "There will be no harm done if you ask her if she would take me for her husband."

The mariners spoke to the fair woman when she came amongst them again, asking her if she would marry Maelduin.

Twice over they asked her if she would do this. On the third day she said, "To-morrow you shall have your answer." The slept then, and when the morning broke they were in a different place from the fortress they had lain down in; they were on their own ship, and they were out at sea, and, no matter in what direction they looked, there was no sign of the island nor of the fortress.

The Shouting Birds, the Pedestal, and the Island of the Mill

They sailed on, and after many days they came to another island. As they drew near it they heard great shouting are chanting, and they were sure that the island was full of human folk. But what they saw on the island was a great multitude of birds, black birds and brown birds and speckled birds, and they were all shouting and chanting. The mariners were deafened by the din the birds made. They did not land on that island; they sailed away again. And on another island near they saw animals like horses that bit each other in the sides, screaming as they did so, and the whole of that island ran with blood. And from that island, too, they sail away. After they had sailed on for a while they came to an island that stood upon a pedestal—it stood as it were upon foot that stood upon the bottom of the sea. In the base of the pedestal there was a door of iron, closed and locked. They tried to open this door, but they tried in vain; they could n open it. And then they sailed away, having seen no one and spoken to no one.

And then they came to an island that had on it a heath. They landed there. In the middle of the heath stood a great and grim-looking mill. They went into it. The miller was here, a giant. He was grinding corn, and the mariners were astonished at the quantity of corn that went into that mill. The giant miller said to them, "All the corn that the men in your country grudge to their neighbors comes here to be ground. Half the corn of your country comes here, for half of it is begrudged." They watched the mill working, and they saw the corn that was ground being carried westward. They crossed themselves in prayer, and went down to their ship, and they sailed away.

The Island of the Mourning Folk and the Island of the Laughing Folk

After that they came to an island that was filled with people; all of them were in black garments, and all were weeping and lamenting. One of the two foster-brothers who were with Maelduin went upon that island. The clothes he wore became black; then he went with the others, weeping and lamenting like them. Two of the mariners went to fetch him; no sooner did they go upon the island than they became black-clad, mourning people. Then Maelduin ordered two more to go fetch these two.

Wrapping their heads in cloths that they might not look upon the land nor breathe the air of the place, the two men went upon the island. They seized the two mariners and they carried them back to the ship. But Maelduin's foster-brother they were not able to seize. Then the vessel had to put off and sail away from that island, for the air of the place made all the mariners sad and regretful. And the two who had gone with the mourning people were not able to tell what had happened to them to make them go through the island weeping and lamenting.

They came to another island—to an island on which there were people who played and laughed incessantly. And there the mariners drew lots as to who should go upon the island; the lot fell to the remaining foster-brother of Maelduin. He went upon the island, and immediately he began to laugh and play like the others. They called to him from the ship, but he gave no heed to their calls. And Maelduin had to order the mariners to sail off, leaving upon the Island of the Laughing Folk the last of his foster-brothers.

The Island of the Eagle

It was after this that they came to the Island of the Eagle. It was a large island, with woods of oak and yew on one side of it, and on the other side a plain on which grazed herds of sheep, and in which there was a little lake. They stayed there for a season, killing the sheep, the meat of which they ate.

It happened that one day they saw what seemed to them to be a cloud coming up from the southwest. As it drew near they beheld the quiver of wings, and they knew that what was over them was an enormous bird. Very wearily great bird alighted on a hill that was in the center of the island; it had carried a branch that had red berries upon it, and it began eating from the branch.

The mariners were fearful that this great bird would seize them in its talons and carry them away. They went

The great bird gave no sign that it had seen him.

into the woods so that its gaze might not be upon them, and they watched it from the place where they hid themselves. And saw that as the fragments of the berries that the bird ate fell into the lake they reddened the water.

Then, after a while, Maelduin came out of hiding, and he went to the foot of the hill on which the great bird rested. It gave no sign that it had seen him. The others came forth, each carrying his shield before him. And then one of the mariners went near to where the great bird was; he even gathered some berries off the branch that the bird had carried from overseas; still it did not regard him. And watching it now the mariners saw that the bird was very old, and that its plumage was dull and decayed.

When it was full noon two birds lesser in size than the first came flying from the south-west; they alighted before the great bird. After they had rested a while they began cleaning and picking off the insects that were on the great bird around its jaws and its eyes. This they continued doing until twilight came; the three birds then ate of the berries.

The next day, when the great bird had been cleaned by the others, it plunged into the lake, and when it had come forth again, the other birds went to it and cleaned it as before, Then, till third day, the great bird remained preening its feathers and shaking its pinions; the mariners saw that its feathers had become glossy. Soaring upwards it flew thrice around the island, and then away to the quarter whence it had come, and its flight was swift and strong. Maelduin and his companions knew that they had looked upon the renewal of the youth of the eagle, as is spoken of in Holy Writ, "Thy youth is renewed like the eagle's."

After they had seen this happening, and after the other two birds had flown away, Diuran the poet, said, "Let us, too, bathe in the lake and renew ourselves as the great bird hath renewed itself." "Nay," the others said, "for the bird may have left much venom in the water." The others would not go into the lake; Diuran plunged into it by himself, and drank of its water. Great vigour came to him from that bathing and from that draught; his eyes were strong and keen for as long as he lived, and not a tooth fell from his jaw, nor a hair from his head, and he never had illness nor any infirmity.

The Island of the Women

They sailed away from the Island of the Eagle, and they came to another island where they landed, drawing their boat up on the beach. Upon that island there was a great earthen rampart that enclosed a white mansion. They went upon the rampart. From where they were they saw maidens, seventeen of them, and they were preparing a bath. In a while a rider came up, riding swiftly upon a horse, and alighted and went within the mansion, while one of the maidens took charge of the horse. Afterwards the rider (they saw that it was a woman) went into the bath. The mariners were seen by the people of the mansion, and one of the maidens came to where they were; she bade them enter the enclosure, saying, "The queen invites you." Maelduin and his companions went within. They bathed, and then sat down to meat, each man with one of the maidens opposite him, and the queen sat opposite Maelduin.

That night the mariners said to Maelduin, "Why should you not marry the queen and gain this island for us as an abiding-place? We are tired of wandering, and it is plain to us that we will never win back to our native land." Thereupon Maelduin spoke to the queen, and she agreed to marry him, and each of the maidens agreed to wed with one of the mariners. So Maelduin and his companions settled upon the island, and they lived there in contentment for a while.

Each day the queen went out of the enclosure to judge the folk who were in the interior of the island, and she returned in the evening. "Stay here, and old age will never fall upon you," she said to Maelduin; "stay here and you and your companions shall remain as you are now for all time. And be no longer wandering about from island to island," she said to him.

When she said this, it seemed good to Maelduin and his companions. But after they had been there for a season, the time began to seem long to them; they wearied of the island, and they longed to have the search for home begun again. Then they spoke to Maelduin and asked him to start on the voyage for their own land. But he said to them, "What shall we find in our own country that is better than what we have here?"

Still they murmured and complained. "Great is Maelduin's love for the queen," they said, "he will give no thought to us who for his sake came so far away from our own land and our own people." And they said again, "Well, let him stay with the queen if he will, but we will leave this island and go back to our own country." Then they went to their boat. Maelduin would not be left behind, and he followed the mariners.

This was while the queen was away judging the folk. They put out to sea in their vessel. But before they had gone far the queen came riding up on her swift horse. She had a ball of twine in her hand, and she flung it after the mariners. Maelduin caught it in his hand. It clung to his hand so that he could not free himself, and the queen, holding the other end, drew the men and the vessel back to the island. Then there was rejoicing amongst the seventeen maidens who all this time had been lamenting.

They stayed on the island for another season. Again the mariners induced Maelduin to go on board the vessel and to put off from the island. And again the queen came riding up and threw the twine which Maelduin caught and which clung to his hand. Again the men and the vessel were drawn back to the island, and again all the maidens rejoiced. After that the mariners said that Maelduin allowed himself to be held and to be drawn back because of his love for the queen. And when they went on board the vessel for the third time, and when the queen rode up and cast the ball of twine, one of the mariners caught it. It clung to his hand as it had clung to Maelduin's. But Diuran the poet drew his sword and smote off the hand of the man, and the hand and the twine that clung to it fell into the sea. The queen, when she saw this happening, began to wail and shriek, and the maidens wailed and shrieked with her, and all the land became a cry and a wail. But the mariners sailed away. And thus they made their escape from the Island of the Women.

The Sea of Glass and the Sea of Mist

And after they had left that island they entered on a sea that was clear and transparent; it was like a sea of green glass. Such was the clearness of that sea that the gravel and sand at the bottom were clearly visible through it; they saw no monsters nor sea-beasts amongst its crags; they saw only gravel and green sand. They voyaged over that wonderful sea, wondering all the time at its splendour and its beauty. They sailed through the green transparent sea, and they came into a sea that was like mist.

They thought that this mist-like sea could not hold up their vessel. Nevertheless, they sailed on and over it. In its depths they saw fortresses, and they saw fair land around the fortresses. And once, beneath them, they saw a monstrous beast in a growing tree; droves of grazing cattle were below that beast, and there was an armed warrior guarding the cattle. But in spite of all the warrior could do, the beast every now and then stretched down a long neck, and seized one cattle and devoured it. The mariners feared that the beast might see them and draw them and their boat down through the mist-like sea.

And as they sailed on they came to a place where, looking down, they saw a throng of people. And the people, them, screamed at them, "It is they, it is they!" Then came a woman who pelted them with nuts from below; the nuts were very large, and the mariners gathered them and took them with them. And as they sailed on they heard the folk below crying to each other,

"Where are they now?" "They are gone away!" "They are not gone!" "It is likely," Diuran the poet said, "that this people knew of a prophecy that said that a people would come and take their country from them, and they think we are that people."

The Silver Column in the Sea, and the Island of the Flaming Rampart

And when they had sailed through the mist-like sea they came to where a silver column rose up from the sea. Very wonderful was that column. It was four-square, and each of the four sides of it was as wide as two oar-strokes of the boat. Not a sod of earth was at its foot, but it rose from the boundless ocean, and its summit was lost in the sky. And from the summit a vast silver net was flung, a net that went far into the sea. Through a mesh of the net their boat sailed.

And as they sailed through it, Diuran the poet drew his sword and hacked at the mesh of the net. "Destroy it not," cried Maelduin, "for what we see is the work of mighty men." But Diuran said, "For the praise of God's name do I this, that our tale of wonder may be believed; if I reach home this piece of silver shall be offered by me on the high altar of Armagh." So he hacked at the mesh and cut a great piece off. They heard a voice from the summit of the column, a voice mighty, clear, and

The flaming ramparts circled round and round the island.

distinct. But they knew not the tongue it spake, or the words it uttered.

And beyond the column they came in sight of an island that had about it a rampart of flame. The flaming rampart circled round and round continually. In one part of it there was an opening, and when this opening came opposite them the mariners saw through it the whole island, and they saw those who dwelt therein, men and women: beautiful beings they were, wearing adorned garments, and with vessels of gold in their hands. And festal music came through that opening to the ears of the voyagers. For a long time they lingered there watching that marvel, and they deemed it all delightful to behold.

The Islands in the Seas of Home

Later on they came to an island with many woods in it, and with birds in the woods. On this island was a solitary man, an anchorite, whose only clothing was his hair, and to whom otters brought salmon out of the sea. The anchorite, when the mariners came to him, prophesied to them, saying, "You will reach your own country, and the man who slew thy father, O Maelduin, you will find in a fortress that you will come to. Slay him not, but forgive him, seeing that God has brought you and your companions through many great perils, although you, too, are men deserving of death." They stayed with the anchorite for three days, and then they sailed away from that island refreshed and greatly heartened by what the anchorite had told them.

They came to an island that looked to them like an island off their homeland. On that island one of the men saw a falcon. "That falcon," he said to Maelduin, "is like the falcons of our own country." "Watch it," Maelduin said, "and see how it flies when it goes from this island." They watched it, and the falcon flew towards the northeast, and they rowed in that direction in which it flew.

At nightfall they sighted land; they came to two bare islands. There was a fortress on each of the islands, and as they drew near to one of them they heard the speech of men within, sitting at meat. One man said:

"It would be ill for us if Maelduin were to come upon us now."

"Maelduin has been drowned," said another man.

"Maybe it is he who shall awaken you from your sleep tonight," said a third man, "awaken you who slew his father."

"If he should come now," said the fourth man, "what should we do?"

"Not hard to answer that," said the one who had slain Maelduin's father, "if he should come here a great welcome we should give him, for he hath been long in great tribulations."

Then Maelduin smote with the wooden clapper

upon the door of the fortress. "Who is there?" said the men within.

"Maelduin is here," said he.

Then he and his companions entered the fortress; they entered it in peace, and a welcome was given them. The garments that they wore and that were now filled with the brine of the sea were taken off them, and new garments were given them. They told the story of all the marvels that God had shown them. And Maelduin and the man who had killed his father kissed each other in peace and forgiveness.

After that Maelduin went back to his home and his kindred in Arran, and Diuran the poet took with him the piece of silver that he had hewn from the net of the column in the sea, and he laid it on the high altar of Armagh, in triumph and exultation at the miracles God had wrought for them. And again they told the story of all that had befallen them, and all the marvels they had seen by sea and land and the perils they had endured. And the chief sage of Ireland wrote the story down, and he did so for a delight of mind, and for the sake of the folk who would come after him.

A monk, clad in white, who sat alone, was called upon by Prince Henry. He rose up and went and stood upon the rostrum; in his hands was a book that had bright pictures alongside its writing—pictures of ships and fishes and strange beasts. The white-clad monk saluted the prince, and to him and to the captains and learned men he spoke, reading to them in a changeless voice out of the book that he held in his hands. It was thus that those who had come together in the tower above the ocean heard:

THE VOYAGES OF SAINT BRENDAN

When he was being baptized a white mist came up from the sea and enfolded all those who were at the well of his baptism. For that he was named Brendan, which means Broen Finn or White Mist.

And he who was named from that which came up from the sea grew up beside the sea, knowing the men who put off from the western coast, and often going out with them in their little vessels. Then, that he might be with great saints and great teachers, he left his home by the sea. He grew in saintliness, and when he had come into his manhood he longed to leave his country and his parents so that he might have no thought with him but the thought of God. He longed to be in some strange and empty land where his thought of God might be deep and clear. And then, one day, he heard a voice from heaven that said to him, "Arise, Brendan, for God will grant thee what thou hast prayed for, and it will be given thee to come into a strange and unknown land."

After that Brendan went back to the place where he was born, the place beside the western sea. He went to the top of the mountain that is called Slieve Daidche, and he built himself a cell there, and there he lived. From his cell on the top of the mountain he could look down upon the wide western ocean, Often he had the vision of a noble and beautiful land beyond the waters. He lived there on the top of the mountain with the sea before him until once again he heard the voice of the angel. And the voice said to him, "It will be shown to thee how to find the land of which thou hast had the vision."

Brendan wept for joy. He went down from his cell on the mountain, and he went and lived amongst men who had come from a race of mariners. After he had been with them for a while, and after he had told them of his vision of a land beyond the ocean, he said to them, "Have three vessels made, the largest vessels that you have ever built, with three banks of oars on each, and with sails of hide, and find twenty men for each vessel." The vessels were made, of the kind that are called currachs, with tanned hides covering a body of wicker-work. Sixty men were found ready to sail with Brendan, some of them mariners and some of them monks. And in vessels that were covered with tanned hides and that had sails of hide, Brendan, with his sixty companions, put off from the western coast and sailed out across the western ocean.

The First Voyage to the Inaccessible Island

They sailed over the loud-voiced waves of the rough-crested sea, and over the billows of the greenish tide, and over the abysses of the wonderful, terrible, relentless ocean, where, looking down, they saw in the depths the red-mouthed monsters of the sea and many great whales. And Brendan said a prayer to God, saying, "O Almighty Creator, who, out of shapeless matter, formed all things and creatures in their proper forms and species, deliver us and bring us safely back across the sea." And when he had said that prayer the sea grew calm and the rushing of the whirlpools subsided at once.

Now as they sailed on across the ocean, having visited many empty islands, the monks who were with him said to Brendan, "It is time that we should make a landing, for Easter is near, and we should come forth from our ships to celebrate the rising of Our Lord." When they said that there was no land in sight.

The next day was Easter. The monks looked around, and they all lamented that there was no land upon which they might celebrate the Lord's resurrection. Then, behold! amongst the billows they saw firm land, land that was like a green sward that is smooth and even and all at the one level. They went to it, and they went upon it. They celebrated the Easter festival upon it for one day and two nights; then they went back to their vessels.

And as they sailed away the level land on which they had been plunged down into the billows and sank into the sea. Then they knew that what they had been on was not a smooth, green island, but was the back of a great whale. For five years Saint Brendan and his companions were upon the ocean, and at every Easter that whale rose out of the ocean and they celebrated Easter upon its bulk.

They sailed on and on towards the west. One day in the trough of the waves, they found a maiden drifting: she was whiter than snow or the foam of the seas, and she was of a size greater than any woman they had ever looked upon; she was a maiden of a giant race. She was dead, being pierced through the body by a spear. Brendan took her within his currach. He prayed over her, and life came back for a while to the maiden. In a language that he only understood, she told Brendan that she was of the people of the Isles of the Sea. Brendan baptized her and administered the sacrament to her; she breathed forth her spirit then. The monks prayed over that mighty maiden, and then they buried her body in the sea.

Still they sailed westward. They came to a small and beautiful island that had many bays that were well supplied with fish. They landed, thinking to rest there and then to sail farther on and to the land that the heavenly voice spoke of to Brendan. Upon that island they found a church built of stone. Brendan and his companions were greatly astonished, for they thought that no one had ever been on the island before them. They searched all over the place. Then, beside a well, Brendan and his companions found an ancient man. He was naked, and he seemed to be without flesh or blood, for his skin was shriveled on his bones. This was the Hermit of the Far Island. He rose up, and he spoke to Brendan and his companions in a language that they understood. He told them that the land they were in search of was the Radiant Land, and that it was still far from them, to the west. And he told them, too, that the currachs they had could not make the voyage to the Radiant Land.

For a while they stayed on the Island of the Ancient

Hermit; then they boarded their vessels once more, and they rowed with their banks of oars and they sailed with their leathern sails until they came to another island. It was an island walled by cliffs so steep that no one could land on it. They saw towers on this inaccessible island, and they heard voices that seemed to be the chanting of men. The chanting lulled the mariners to sleep. Again and again they sailed around the island, trying to find a landing-place, but they found none. At length, from a tower on the top of the cliffs, a waxen tablet was let down to them. They read words written upon that tablet, and the words were, "Waste no time or toil in striving to come upon this island, for you cannot come upon it. The land you are in quest of you will come to by another way." When they read that Brendan and his companions turned from the Inaccessible Island, and in their currachs they sailed back to Ireland. But in Brendan's mind was the resolve to go forth on another time, and to voyage on until he came to that Radiant Land that the hermit by the well had spoken to him about.

Brendan Prepares for His Second Voyage

After Brendan had returned and had dwelt a while in his own country, he resolved to go into Britain so that he might have converse there with wise men and men who had voyaged upon the sea. Gildas the Wise was the

one whom he desired most to have counsel with. He
went and he abode for a while in the monastery that
Gildas was the head of.

Now one day Gildas the Wise said to Brendan, his
guest. "There are in the wilderness near by two very
powerful and ravenous wolves that attack people and
destroy the flocks and even beset this monastery of ours."
When Brendan heard this he asked leave to go forth
that he might look on the track of the beasts. Then he
went into the wilderness taking with him his disciple,
Talmach. A number of men on horseback followed;
they wanted to see from a distance Brendan's encounter
with the wolves.

As he went on he committed himself entirely to
God, saying to himself, "What is the world to me, or
what do I care for it? I will conquer these beasts that
are destroying the people of this place." He and his
disciple went on and up to the very lair of the beasts.
And there they found the mother wolf asleep with her
young ones in the noonday sun. He had Talmach go
up to her and arouse her gently. She stood up and she
cried her wolf's cry, and her mate came towards her. But
Brendan, unafraid, went between the beasts and spoke
to them, saying, "Follow me now very gently with your
little ones." The men who had followed on horseback
looked on in affright, expecting to see Brendan and

Talmach torn to pieces by the beasts, but instead they saw the beasts following the two men like dogs of the house. Then the men on horseback fled before them.

Gildas was standing at the gate of the town. Seeing Brendan and Talmach coming towards him with the beasts following them, he gave thanks to God for all the wonders He performs. Then, after they had brought them before Gildas, Brendan spoke to the wild beasts, and he bade them go back into the wilderness, and to harm never more the men of that land nor their flocks. The two beasts with their young ones went back; never again did they come near the people nor the place.

Brendan had come into Britain that he might hear of islands beyond their islands, and of how mariners might come to them. There was a youth in Gildas's monastery whose name was Malo; he had sailed in quest of one of the islands in the Western Sea. With his companions he had come to an island where a giant dwelt, a giant whose name was Mildu. From Mildu they learned that there was a great island to the west the name of which was Yma; the giant had seen it, and he told Malo and his companions that it was surrounded by a wall of gold of a great height. And Mildu, being of an enormous size, offered to draw Malo's ship to that island by wading through the sea.

So they went across the sea, Mildu drawing the ship. But a great storm came up, and the dash of the waves broke the cable by which the giant drew the ship. Never again did they see the giant, and they supposed that he had been drowned by the great waves. They came back to his island, and afterwards they sailed for their own land.

Other islands were spoken of, islands that had people of their own kind upon them and that were to the north of Britain. Gildas the Wise agreed that Brendan might go to these islands and preach the gospel of Christ to the people who were upon them.

So with Malo he sailed north, and they came to the far, bleak Orkneys; they built churches there and they preached the gospel to the people. But all the time Brendan's thoughts were upon the lands in the Western Sea, the fair lands that the Hermit in the Far Island had spoken to him about. He left the Orkneys and he came back to Ireland; he visited his foster-mother Ita, and he asked counsel of her as to his going west.

When she heard of the Radiant Land that was known to the Hermit, Ita said, "Such a voyage could never be made in vessels that were held together by the skins of dead beasts. Only a great ship made of clean wood could carry them so far." Then she told Brendan that he would have to go into Connacht, into the western land of Ireland, and have the people build for him the greatest ship that ever sailed out of their bays.

So Brendan went into Connacht. There, after he

had saved the people from invasion and war, he asked them to build for him a ship of wood, a ship that would hold sixty mariners. The people of the west built him such a ship, and they filled it with all that was needful for the longest voyage that men ever made. They gave a shipwright and a smith to go with them on the voyage, so that the vessel might be kept in repair. Then Brendan and his companions made ready to sail.

First they sailed to the island of Arran, where Enda, a saint and a wise man, had brought together a number of pupils and had learned men to teach them. Brendan stayed for a while with Enda, taking counsel with him and with the instructors who were with him. Then Enda blessed Brendan's ship and blessed all who sailed in it. And Brendan, once again, sailed out into the Western Sea.

The Island of the Sheep

Their sail was set towards the summer solstice; they had a fair wind in the beginning; therefore they had no labor except to keep the sail properly set. After twelve days, however, the wind fell to a dead calm; then they had to labor at the oars until their strength was nearly exhausted.

It was in these days that Brendan said to them, "Fear not, brothers, for God will be unto us a helper, a mariner, and a pilot; take in the oars and helm, keep the sail set, and may God do unto us, His servants and His little vessel, as He willeth." They took refreshment always in the evening, and sometimes a wind sprang up, but they knew not from what point it blew, or in what direction it set them sailing.

It was then that they saw that monster of the deep, whose name, as it was revealed to Brendan, is Jasconius. "This is the largest of all the fish that swim in the ocean," Brendan said. "It is ever trying to make its head and tail meet, but it cannot succeed, because of its great length."

Afterwards they came in view of an island towards which they sailed with a favorable wind. When the boat touched on the landing-place, Brendan ordered all to disembark, he being the last to leave the boat. They went across the island; on their way they saw great streams of water flowing from many fountains, full of all kinds of fish.

On that island there were flocks of sheep, all pure white, and so numerous as to hide the face of the land. Now it was near Easter, and Brendan said to his companions, "Let us celebrate Easter here, and, as this is the festival of the Lord's Supper, let us eat a lamb in memory of it." Upon his saying this they took from the flock a spotless lamb, which, being tied around the neck, followed at their heels as if it were a pet. Then there came to them a man who saluted Brendan and rejoiced that they had taken a lamb from his flock for the Paschal Feast; he brought them a basket of hearth-cakes, and he showed them a place that was suitable for the celebration of Easter.

Then Brendan, looking upon the flocks, asked the man how it came that his sheep were so large—almost as large as oxen are with us were the sheep of that island. The man told them that they grew to that size because they never were milked and because they always had good pasture, neither they nor the fields ever feeling the stress of bitter winds. When Easter had been celebrated, Brendan and his companions took leave of the man of that island, giving and receiving parting blessings. They went into their vessel; across the sea from the Island of the Sheep they saw another, a smaller island, and they sailed towards it.

The Island of the Cat

Before Brendan sailed these seas three students had come that way in a hide-covered currach. They were youths who had gone out from Ireland on a pilgrimage; ardently they had desired to go some place where they could give themselves completely up to the thought of God. So they had put out to sea in their little vessel, taking nothing with them but three small cakes; one of the students brought with him a little cat that was the pet of the monastery they had lived in.

They had no sail nor oars; they went upon the waves trusting that God would take them to the place where they might serve Him best. Their currach went out into the main sea. Then for days and days they had drifted on; at last they came to that little island that Brendan and his companions saw when they looked across from the Island of the Sheep.

Now when the students landed there they found berries on the trees and roots in the ground; they ate of the berries and roots and they went to build an altar to the Lord who had brought them safely across the sea. And while they were doing this the little cat that had been brought with them went away.

The little cat returned bringing to the students a fine salmon that she had caught. They cooked it and ate it with their berries and roots. And the next day the little cat brought them a salmon just as fine as the one she had caught before. Every twenty-four hours the little cat brought them a salmon to eat with their berries and roots.

After a while one of the students said to the others, "Our pilgrimage which was to have meant for us hardships and hungers for the sake of finding God is now no pilgrimage at all; we, it seems, have brought our cat

The little cat returned bringing a fine salmon.

to feed us, and here, on this island, we have as good fare as ever we have had, through the cat's providing."

After that they resolved that they would eat no more of the salmon that the little cat brought them. Day after day the salmon was laid beside them, and day after day they refused to eat of it, partaking only of their berries and roots.

Then it was revealed to them that the salmon the little cat had brought to them was given them by the mercy of God. They thanked God for the provision He sent, and thereafter they ate the salmon that was brought them.

And now they wanted to give thanks to God for the provision He sent them. Said one of the students, "Let each of us declare what he will do as a thank-offering. For my part I will sing thrice fifty psalms every day together with the Office and the Mass."

Said the second student, "I will say thrice fifty long prayers every day together with the Office and the Mass."

Said the third student, "I will sing thrice fifty hymns every day together with the celebration of the canonical hours and the Mass."

So every day the three students made their thank-offering for the food that was given them on that little island. Then, after a space of time, one of the students died. His requiem was sung by the two who were left and he was buried upon the island. The two students divided between them the thank-offering that their comrade had made; each of them did half of it while keeping up his own thank-offering. One said to the other, "Of a truth the Lord hath a greater love for our brother than for either of us; him He hath taken to Himself and us He hath left behind."

Soon afterwards a second of the students died; he was buried by his comrade who sang the requiem over him. Then the one who was left took it upon himself to make the thank-offering that was made by the three of them.

It came to pass that an angel visited this solitary man. "Thy Lord is angry with thee," the angel said. "He is angry with thee because of thy murmurings; thou dost know that His mercy to thee is constant." "Why, then," said the solitary man, "did He not suffer me to die with my comrades? Why have they been taken to Him, and why have I been left?" "The choice was thine," said the angel. "Thou didst undertake to sing the longest hymns, and for that thou shalt have long life here and see the glory of God hereafter." "A blessing upon the Lord from whom thou hast come. I am thankful to Him," said the solitary man.

And on that island he lived, growing to be a very ancient man. He was there when Brendan came to that island, sailing from the Island of the Sheep. He was there and his cat was with him.

The cat sprang into the sea as Brendan and his companions landed, and it was never seen again as long as they were upon the island. The ancient solitary man told him the story of his coming to the place and the story of those who had been with him. Then Brendan prepared him for his death, and administered the sacrament to him. The ancient solitary man, the last of the three who had come to that far island, departed this life in the presence of Brendan and his companions. The voyagers buried him on the island beside his comrades, and they sang the requiem over him. After that Brendan and his companions sailed away from the Island of the Cat.

Some Wonders of the Ocean

After they had sailed three days from the Island of the Cat, the wind fell; then the sea became like a great curdled mass, so great was the calm. It was then that Brendan said to the mariners, "Take in your oars, and cast loose the sails, for the Lord will guide our vessel whithersoever He willeth." With sails loosed and with oars shipped the vessel drifted through the great curdled mass of the sea. For twenty days they went on in a slow drift, then God sent a favorable wind; the sails took it and the mariners worked their oars, and they went on in a westerly direction, taking refreshment every third day.

One day a fish of enormous size appeared swimming after the vessel; he spouted foam from his nostrils, and he ploughed through the waves in rapid pursuit to devour them. Then the brethren cried out to God, "O Lord who hast made us, deliver us, Thy servants." And to Brendan they cried, "Help, O father, help us." Brendan besought the Lord to deliver them, praying that the monster might not be permitted to devour them, while he also sought to encourage the brethren by these words, "Fear not, you of little faith; for God, who is always our protector, will deliver us from the jaws of this monster, and from every other danger." Then, when the monster was drawing near to them, waves of immense size rushing on before him dashed up on the gunwale of the boat; this caused the brethren to fear more and more. But Brendan, with hands upraised to heaven, earnestly prayed, "Deliver, O Lord, Thy servants, as Thou didst deliver David from the hands of the giant Goliath, and Jonah from the power of the great whale."

While these prayers were being uttered, another monster came into view from the west, and rushing against the other, spouting flame from his mouth, at once attacked it. Then Brendan spoke, "Behold, my children, the wonderful work of our Saviour; await now the end in safety, for this conflict will bring no evil to us, but only greater glory to God." Thereupon the monster that was in pursuit of their ship was slain, and the monster that overcame it returned whence it came.

After that, when Brendan was celebrating the festival of St. Peter in the boat, they found the sea so clear that they could plainly see what was at the bottom. They saw beneath them various monsters of the deep, and so clear was the water, that it seemed as if they could touch with their hands its greatest depths; and the fishes were visible in great shoals, like flocks of sheep in their pastures, swimming around, heads to tails, And there again they saw Jasconius, the largest of all the fishes that swim in the ocean, which is ever trying to make its head and tail meet, but cannot succeed, because of its great length.

Then those who were in the boat entreated Brendan to say his Mass in a low voice, lest those monsters of the deep, hearing the strange voice, might be stirred up to attack them; but Brendan said, "I wonder much at your folly. Why do you dread these monsters?" Having thus spoken, he proceeded to sing Mass in a louder voice, as the brethren were still gazing at the large fishes; and these, when they heard the voice of Brendan, rose up from their depths, and swam around the ship in such numbers, that the brethren could see nothing but the swimming fishes, which, however, came not close to the boat, but swam around at some distance, until Mass was ended, when they swam away in divers directions, out of the view of the brethren. For eight days, with a favorable wind and all sails set, they were scarcely able to pass out of this transparent sea.

One day they saw a column in the sea, which seemed not far off, yet they could not come close to it for three days. When they drew near it, Brendan looked towards its summit, but could not see it, because of its great height and the mists which were about it. It was of the clearest crystal and was as hard as marble. Brendan ordered the brethren to take in their oars, and to lower the sails and mast. When this had been done, he said, "Run in the boat now through an opening, that we may get a closer view of this wonderful work of God." And when they had passed through the opening, enduring great cold as they went through, and looked around them, the sea seemed to them transparent like glass, so that they could plainly see everything beneath them, even to the base of the column.

Brendan then measured the opening between four pavilions, which he found to be four cubits on every side. When they sailed along for a day by one side of the column, they could always feel the shade as well as the heat of the sun, beyond the ninth hour; and after thus sailing about the column for four days, they found the measurement of each side to be four hundred cubits. Next day they rowed towards the north, and having passed out through an opening, they set up the mast, and unfurled the sails again. A favorable wind came on so that they had no occasion to use the oars, but only to hold the ropes and the tiller. And thus for eight days they were borne along towards the north.

The Soul That Was Permitted to Revisit the Earth

One day, as they went towards the north, Brendan and his companions observed a very dense cloud, and, on approaching it, they saw a shape that was like nothing they expected to see upon that cold sea; some of the brethren thought that what they saw was a bird; others thought it was a boat; others, that it was a man. Brendan told them to cease the discussion, and to steer directly for what they saw.

It was Christmas then, and the mariners were bitterly cold. As they came close to what they were steering for they saw that it was a berg of ice, and that there was a man seated upon it. Dread fell upon all of them as they looked upon that man, with his hanging lips and his scowling brow. A rough piece of stone was under him; the waves on every side in their flowing beat upon

"Yes, I am Judas, the most wicked of all traffickers."

him, even to the top of his head, and in their ebbing exposed the bare rock on which he was sitting. And as he looked upon him it was revealed to Brendan who this fearsome being so fearfully positioned was. "Judas," he whispered to his companions, "Judas who has come out of the pit of fire."

Then the one seated upon the iceberg said, "Yes, I am Judas Iscariot, the most wicked of all traffickers. Know that the bitter cold that you feel around you is for me a refreshing coolness, and that it is through the mercy of God that I am permitted to be here. On the day that you celebrate the feast of Our Lord's birth I am permitted to come here.

"The world that you belong to knows of my great crime and knows of the punishment that is due to me because of it. But it does not know of the mercy that has been shown to me. It is for you, Brendan the Holy, to tell men of it.

"Once, in the city of Joppa, I came through a street in which an old man terribly afflicted with leprosy was sitting. He begged of me, as he begged of all the passers-by, to put some covering over his nakedness, for the sand, driven by the wind, was upon his sores. I had many garments then, and I took off my cloak and covered him with it. I went on then, and I gave the leper no other thought.

"And when it came about that I was suffering for the great crime I had wrought, an angel came to me. The angel said, 'Rise up, Judas, out of the pit of fire, and take some respite from your pains.' 'Whence comes this mercy?' I asked. 'It comes from the mercy that thou didst show to the leper in Joppa,' the angel told me.

"Then I went forth—it was on the day of Our Lord's nativity—and into the frozen sea. And on every Christmas Day I am permitted to come here, and the fire in my breast and brain goes from me in these hours, and for one day in the year I have ease of my pain. The stone I sit on was put down by my hands in a rut of a road near Jerusalem that travelers might go more easily upon their way."

Brendan and his companions bowed their heads as they heard of the mercy that had been shown Judas Iscariot. Their ship drifted on. When they looked back again the berg of ice and the figure seated upon it were gone from their sight.

The Island of the Smiths and the Fragrant Island

They heard sounds as of thunder; they heard a din as of iron being beaten heavily; they saw black smoke arising; they sailed on, and they came in sight of an island. Then Brendan said to his mariners, "The sound that we hear as thunder is the sound of bellows being blown; the din that we hear is that of iron being struck on anvils; the smoke that we see is the smoke of many smithies. I name this island the Island of the Smiths, and I pray that no evil will befall us when we come to it."

The mariners hoped that they would be able to land on the island and get provisions from the folk who were there. As they came near it they were nearly deafened by the thunderous sounds of the bellows and the din of iron striking iron, and their eyes were nearly blinded by the bitter black smoke that was blown to them. They saw men upon the island, but as they drew near they saw no place where they might land; all that was before them was black, low-lying rocks.

The men were black, too, and were seemingly begrimed by the smoke that rose up from every part of the island. They came crowding out on the rocks; they were long-armed and broad-shouldered men, but they were stunted in size. And the mariners saw that they had patches of hair upon their bodies.

They shouted from the rocks to the ship. What they shouted was in a tongue unknown to the mariners; they sailed around trying to get a passage through the black rocks. The men dashed away from the shore, shouting to one another.

Brendan counseled the mariners to turn the ship away from that island. But they were weary, and they wanted to rest on land; also they wanted to get fresh provisions for their ship. And although the smoke blown towards them from the smithies blinded their eyes, still they sailed for that shore.

And now the begrimed men came back to the rocks, shouting and making a clamour. It seemed as if all the dwellers on the island were there. Each had a tongs in his hands, the tongs holding a mass of burning iron. One lifted up his tongs with the burning mass in it and flung the fiery iron at the ship. It fell into the water near the vessel, making a hissing and a steaming. Then the mariners were frightened; they put the oars into the water, and they pulled away. The smoke that blew from the island nearly blinded them, and they could hear the hissing all around them as the fiery masses flung at the ship fell into the water. Swiftly they pulled away, and they were lucky that none of the iron flung struck the vessel. Soon they were out of the smoke that blew from the island, and the hissing and the steaming from the fiery masses were around them no more. But until they were very far away they heard the sounds that belonged to that island—the thunderous blowing of the bellows and the din of iron striking upon iron.

They came into a current that drew the ship towards the south and away from the bleak seas on which the bergs of ice floated. Then, one day, a bird of resplendent whiteness flew over the ship. It carried in its beak a branch of a tree; it let the branch fall upon the ship.

It was a branch of an unknown tree, and it was covered with large red berries. The mariners plucked off the berries, and, dividing them amongst themselves, ate of them eagerly, for now they were famishing for want of food. They were strengthened and refreshed by the berries, each of which was as large as a grape.

On and on the ship sailed; at last they came to an island on which they were able to make a landing. There were six fountains upon that island. They anchored the ship and they rested upon the island, and they went through it, but not a single human being, not a single living creature, did they find upon it. Trees grew there, many of them bearing such berries as were upon the branch that the bird had dropped upon their ship. Many of the trees, too, were sweet-smelling. Indeed, so fragrant was the island because of the sweet-smelling trees that Brendan said that it smelled like a house of pomegranates. They named that island the Fragrant Island.

The Paradise of Birds

For many days they rested on the Fragrant Island, refreshing themselves with the fruits that grew on its trees. They took water and fruits to their ship, and then they sailed away.

They sailed on until they came to an island that had a

"All the companies of birds," he said, "were once angels."

river flowing from it, a river that mingled its water with the water of the sea. They sailed up that river, going along while the banks narrowed upon them until their ship almost touched either bank. Up the river they went, going on until they could go no farther. They saw from where they stayed a fountain, and growing over the fountain, a great, wide tree.

That tree had many branches, and the branches were all glistening with green leaves. It was wonderful, that tree. But more wonderful than the tree with its green and glistening leaves were the birds that rested upon it—companies and companies of birds, each bird being of a marvelous whiteness.

And as Brendan looked upon that wonderful tree with the wonderful companies of birds upon it, an overmastering desire to know why the birds were there, and where they had come from possessed him, and he besought God to let him know what was the meaning of it all. As he prayed one of the birds flew from the glistening tree and perched itself upon the prow of the ship, spreading out its wings. Again Brendan besought God to let him know the reason for the birds being there. Then, even as his prayer ended, the bird spoke in a human voice and with human words to Brendan. "All the companies of birds that are upon the glistening tree," it said, "were once angels serving the most high God.

When the great host of angels fell from heaven we were not with those who fell. But we were not with those who remained faithful to God, doing His will. And because we were not with the faithful ones we might not remain in heaven. And because we were not with the unfaithful ones God's mercy would not condemn us to the pit of fire. So we remain between the heavens and the earth. It is permitted to us to stay on the island and sing the praises of the Creator."

As the bird on the prow of the ship said this, all the companies of birds on the branches of the green glistening tree lifted up their voices and sang a hymn in the Creator's praise, a hymn so wonderful that Brendan and all the mariners with him wept to hear it. Every day the companies of birds sang this hymn.

Until Pentecost the mariners stayed on the island that Brendan named the Paradise of Birds, and they were filled with the marvel of that singing, and of the whiteness of the birds in the green glistening branches of that wonderful tree. At Pentecost the mariners departed from that island, taking with them water and fruits.

The Island of the Anchorites

They sailed on for forty days, and they came then to an island around which there were high cliffs. They were glad to come to that island, but they could find no creek nor harbor into which their ship might go. Around the island with its unbroken cliffs they sailed until they were nearly dead with weariness.

As last they saw a figure standing on a cliff, the figure of a man; he motioned them to take a certain course. They took that course and they came to a narrow passage between cliffs through which they were able to steer their ship. They landed at the end of that channel. Near where they landed there was two wells of water, one stagnant, and the other clear and limpid. They went to the clear well and refreshed themselves from its water.

And as they were there an ancient man approached them; so ancient was he that his hair was as white as snow and his face was of a transparent whiteness. He motioned to the mariners to follow him. He brought them to where there were many small buildings of stone with a large building set beside them.

Then Brendan knew that they had come upon an island on which anchorites or hermits lived: these buildings were their cells and their church. The anchorites spoke neither to the mariners nor to one another, but they made signs, and their signs were understood by Brendan.

They gave the mariners a place to rest in, and they brought them food that was nourishing and sustaining. Brendan and his companions stayed on, and they soon

A fiery arrow flew over each lamp and lit it.

came to understand all that the anchorites would have them understand.

The church that they had built was a wonderful one: in form it was a perfect square, its four walls being each the very same length. There were seven lamps in that church; three hanging before the altar, and one in the middle of each of the walls. The lamps were wonderful, too. Each lamp was of the clearest crystal, and the light in each burned bright and clear.

Brendan wondered how these seven crystal lamps were lighted. The ancient man knew of Brendan's desire to know about the lighting of the lamps, and he signed to him to wait in the church and watch for their lighting.

Night came, and the lights in the crystal lamps sank down: Brendan watched to see how they would be relighted. As he watched a fiery arrow came through a window-opening; as it passed over each lamp before the altar it lit it, so that the lights became bright and clear again. And an arrow flew along each wall, and made the lamp that was there become bright again. So the crystal lamps burned again brightly in the church, and Brendan rejoiced that he was permitted to see the wonder of the lighting of them.

The ancient man knew of the search that Brendan and his mariners were upon—the search for the Radiant Land. He wrote down on a tablet what they were to do so that they might come to that land that lay far west of them. They had to sail far and fare through strange happenings; then if their faith remained strong and their courage high they would come to the Radiant Land.

The Radiant Land

They took the provision that they gave them—roots and fruits and water and bread—and they sailed away from the Anchorites' Island, rejoicing that their course was now towards the Radiant Land. For forty days they sailed on, and then the happening that the ancient man had foreshown them came upon them.

A dark cloud came up and overshadowed the ship. It made a darkness in which they could not see one another, nor see the ocean they sailed through. On and on they sailed, the mariners groping their way about the ship. They knew they were nearing the Radiant Land, but the way towards it was being hidden from them, as the ancient man had foreshown them. Then the dark cloud passed. Brightness was around them once more, and Brendan and his companions looked upon the land of their search, looked upon the Radiant Land.

It was not an island; before them, on each side, a long line of land stretched away. Bright sun was shining upon that land, and all on it seemed fair and good to the mariners. They brought their ship into an inlet of the land, and then they went upon it. Fair trees grew there; vines grew from the trees, and there were grapes upon the vines. They went through that land singing hymns in praise of God who had brought them there in safety; they went on for many days, and they saw no men in all the land.

As they crossed the land from east to west, they came to where a great river flowed down through the land. It was wide and they were not able to cross it. Then as they stood there a figure came towards them; it was the figure of a youth, in semblance like other youths they had known, but with something shining in his presence. And speaking to the mariners in a language that they understood, he told them that the river was the boundary fixed for them, and that they were not to cross it. Brendan then asked the youth if any that would come after him might cross that river, and the youth said that in God's time men would come to where they had come and would cross that wide-flung river.

Brendan and his mariners turned from the river. They crossed the land from east to west and came to where their ship was. They took provision of the fruits and grain of the land, and water, and they sailed away. The cloud once more overshadowed their ship, and for many days they went on through darkness. Then, once more they saw the ocean around them; they sailed on from west to east, touching at certain islands, and at last they came back to the country that they had sailed from. And so it was that Brendan and his companions came to the Radiant Land and returned from it after many years.

The white-garmented monk ceased speaking, and, closing the book with the bright pictures he came down amongst the captains and the wise men.

He whom Prince Henry next called upon was an old, but tall, upright, and broad-shouldered man, with long curling hair of the whiteness of lint. When he stood upon the rostrum that was the prow of an ancient ship, there was that about him that made all who were there think of hailing him as a king of the sea. Very stately he stood before all, tall, white-haired, unbending, and in a voice that was slow and very deep he told them of the voyages and explorations of:

THE CHILDREN OF ERIC THE RED

Leif the Lucky

There was once a young man named Leif, who was a great mariner. He sailed from the Hebrides on a certain year and came to Norway, and there he was received by the king who was ruling at that time, King Olaf. Now Olaf had become a Christian, and he was anxious to have all who were of the Norse race turn from being pagan and become Christian. So he asked young Leif to go into Greenland, and proclaim Christianity to the people there, and also to bring a priest on his ship to them.

Leif, the young seaman, laughed. "No one you could find is more fitted to do this than I am," he told the king. "It was my father, Eric the Red, who first went into Greenland, and named it, and brought settlers into it from Iceland. And my father is still the chief man in Greenland. But," he said, "my father is of the old pagan faith, and he will not relish my striving to change that faith in his own settlement. I'll carry over the priest, however, and I'll proclaim Christianity in Greenland."

So Leif left Norway, taking the priest on his ship, and he sailed towards that land that his father had been the first to go upon and bring settlers to. Eric the Red had named the land Greenland. It was really a land of icy mountains, but he thought and he said that people would be more likely to come and settle in it with him if he gave it a pleasant name. And so he called it Greenland.

On his voyage from Norway Leif came upon a wrecked ship, and he took the people and the cargo off it, and he managed to bring the ship along. The ship and the cargo became his, and so he came to Greenland with great gains. And for this he was known ever afterwards as Leif the Lucky.

He came to Brattahlid, his father's place, and he was well received by all the settlers. His father, old Eric the Red, said that the gain he had brought to them through saving the ship and the cargo was over-balanced by his bringing an impostor amongst them. By impostor he meant the priest King Olaf had sent. However, Leif proclaimed Christianity in Greenland, and nearly all the people there accepted it.

Leif now lived at his father's house in Brattahlid; Thorwald and Thorstein, his brothers, lived there also, and his sister, whose name was Freydis. Now after he had been a while there he said to his father, the old voyager, "Are there, do you think, any new lands that a man might come to and settle in as you came to and settled in Greenland?" "I have a notion that there are," his father said. "I have heard talk of a man named Biarni, and of how he came into sight of lands farther west than this. But this Biarni doesn't seem to have had the spirit to go to and explore them."

Biarni, it happened, came into Greenland that summer. Leif sought him out, and asked him to tell him about the lands he had seen. Thereupon the other gave him a full account of them. Leif then bought a ship from Biarni, and he collected a crew of thirty-five men, and he made ready for a voyage towards the place where Biarni had sighted the unnoted lands.

He asked Eric the Red, that famous old voyager, to become the leader of the expedition. At first Eric said that he was too stricken in years to head such an expedition, and that he was not as well able to endure the labors of sea-life as he had been. But Leif persuaded him, telling him that no man would be more likely than he to bring good fortune to voyaging and seeking men. And at last he persuaded his father to go with them.

They put little cargo on the ship; indeed they took nothing on it except their weapons and provisions for the voyage. Old Eric was to come to them when the ship was ready to make sail. On that morning he took out a chest that held his silver and gold and he hid it a little way from his house. Then he mounted his horse to ride down to the beach. But his horse stumbled and threw him off, and his fall injured his back and leg. "It is not ordained for me to discover any more lands," said Eric the Red, "and where I am I will abide." Thereupon he returned to Brattahlid, and Leif, his son, took charge of the ship.

They sailed in the direction that Biarni had given them, and they came first to the land that he had seen last. There was no grass on that land; great ice mountains lay inland of it, and there was a table-land of flat rock all the way from the sea to the ice mountain. "This is not a land for us," said Leif. "However, we will give it a name." And he named it Helluland from the flat stones that were on it.

They sailed south from Helluland, and they came to a second land; it was wooded, and there were great stretches of white sand where it was level by the sea.

"This land shall be given a name too," said Leif, and he named it Markland from the woods that were upon it.

They had landed on Markland, and afterwards, sailing southward, they came to an island that was off a mainland. There they went ashore and wandered about. There was dew upon the grass there, and they put their hands down and gathered the dew with their hands and put it to their mouths; it seemed to them that never before in their whole lives had they tasted anything so sweet and so refreshing as this dew was. Then they put to sea again.

They sailed into a sound that was between the island and a cape which ran out to the eastward of the land; then they sailed westward past the cape. At ebb-tide there were broad reaches of shallow water there and their ship grounded. They did not wait for the tide to float her, so anxious were they to get to the land, but they went off the ship and they dashed across the reaches to the land. A river flowed out of a lake at the place. Afterwards they went back to the ship, and as soon as the tide rose beneath her they floated her up the river and thence into the lake. There they cast anchor. They went ashore, taking their hammocks with them. And in that place they built their huts and they settled down.

Their ship was secure, and they resolved to stay in the land beside the lake for the winter. They built a large house, making themselves comfortable there. There were salmon in the river and the lake—larger salmon than they had ever seen before—and they were easily able to take them. The grass hardly withered in the winter, and they saw that cattle could graze there without having to be foddered. The days and nights were of more equal length than they were in Iceland and Greenland.

When the house had been built, Leif divided his men into two parties; one went exploring the country while the other remained near the house, catching game and preparing the meals. Alternately each party did these things. Leif ordered the exploring party not to go so far but that they could return to the house the same evening, and not to separate from each other. At times Leif joined the exploring party and at times he remained at the house.

There was a man named Tyrker with the crew. He was not a seaman; he was a very expert craftsman, and he had been so long in his father's house that Leif looked upon him as his foster-father. This man separated from the exploring party one day, and he did not return to the house that evening. This made Leif very anxious. He got together a party of twelve men and they went in search of Tyrker. They had not gone very far when they saw the man coming towards them, and they shouted out a welcome to him.

Tyrker was an undersized individual, with a prominent forehead and quick-moving eyes. As Leif watched him coming towards them he saw that his foster-father was grinning and mumbling and rolling his eyes about. "Wherefore art thou so belated?" asked Leif. Tyrker stood grinning there and nodding his head. Then as they came up to him he began to throw out words in his own language, in German. Leif could not understand what he said nor what had happened to him, and he laid his hand upon his shoulder and shook him. Then Tyrker, grinning still, spoke to them in the Norse language. "I haven't been much farther away than the rest of you," he said, "but I have found something that has made it worth while to come here." "What have you found, foster-father?" "Something that is in my own country and not in yours." Thereupon he led them to a place and showed them grapes growing. "Grapes that wine is made from," he said, grinning again. Leif and his men were overjoyed to see the fruit that they had often been told of growing there. The grapes were in great abundance, and the men came and took bunches from the vines. They brought heaps of grapes to the ship. Also they made wine there.

They cut trees down and loaded them on the ship, making a cargo of them, for timber was scarce and valuable in Greenland. And in the woods they found something very valuable. Many trees there had great knobs or warts upon them. This was mösur wood. It could be wrought into thin forms that would not crack or split and so made into handsome bowls and cups and goblets.

This mösur wood growing so plentifully on the trees there was a great find for Leif the Lucky. He and his men gathered much of it. Then, when the winter was over, they brought their ship with its cargo out of that lake. Before that Leif had named the land they had tarried in: because of the grapes they had found there he named it Wineland the Good.

They took the homeward course, and they sailed on with fair winds until they sighted Greenland and the fells below its glaciers. They brought their ship into the harbor they had sailed from, and they went to Brattahlid where Eric the Red was, with his sons Thorwald and Thorstein, and his daughter Freydis. Leif had much profit from the cargo he brought back, and he had fame on account of his voyage, and the land that he had named Wineland the Good was much spoken about thereafter in Greenland and Iceland.

Thorwald, Eric's Second Son

The next thing that happened was that Thorwald, Leif's brother, wanted to make the voyage to Wineland the Good for the sake of the profit that was in it. Leif gave him his ship, and Eric's second son gathered together a crew of thirty men. They put the ship in order, and they set out, but there is no record of their voyage until they came to where Leif had made his landing. They went up the river and into the lake, and they found Leif's huts still standing. Their ship they laid up and they passed the winter there, supporting themselves on the fish they caught in the river and the lake.

Spring came on, and Thorwald ordered a party of his men to take the ship's boat and explore along the western coast. This they did, and they found a region that was very fair and wooded down to the water's edge. But no house of man nor den of beast was there to be seen. They spent the summer making this exploration, and when autumn came they turned back; they entered the lake, and they passed another winter by the huts that Leif had left.

They got together a cargo of timber and mösur wood, and then when the summer came again Thorwald had the ship put in readiness, and the whole party went voyaging in the ship. They sailed eastward and around the land to the northward. They came to a place where a headland went into the sea, a headland that was all covered with trees. There was good anchorage there, and they took the ship in, and they put out a gang-plank, and Thorwald and his companions went upon the land, a land that Leif had not been on.

And so pleasant was that land that Thorwald said to his friends, "This is a lovely land, and I would fain have my home here." Then, with his friends, he went along the sand, going back to the ship. They came upon what seemed to them three mounds upon the sand: going up to them they found that they were three canoes upturned, with three men under each. And so it was that they came upon the men of that land.

The men were asleep, and Thorwald and his party captured eight of them. One escaped and fled away. Then Thorwald and his companions went up on the headland; they saw clumps upon the ground, and they knew that these were the dwellings of the natives of the place. They went back to the ship that was drawn up on the beach, and some of them lay down on the sand and some of them on the deck, and so great was their drowsiness that they all fell asleep.

They were all awakened by a great cry that seemed to come from above them: "Wake thou, Thorwald! Thou and all thy companions! " They all sprang up awake, and, looking out on the water, they saw a great number of canoes coming towards them.

The natives in the canoes shouted, and they shot arrows and stones at them. "We will put out the ship-shield, and we will defend ourselves as well as we can," Thorwald said. The fight was not for long, for the

Skraelings, as the men in the ship named the people in the canoes, soon drew away. Then said Thorwald, speaking to his men, "Have any of you been wounded?" They answered saying that none of them had been given a hurt. "That is well," said Thorwald. "But I have been wounded in the arm-pit; an arrow flew between the edge of the ship and the shield, in under my arm. Here is the arrow, and it will prove a mortal wound to me. Now hear my counsel: make the ship ready and depart from this place instantly. But before you sail away, take me to the place that I thought it best to abide in, and bury me there, so that the words that I said may be made true— that it will be my dwelling-place. And place a cross at my head and another at my feet, and name the place Crossness on account of my being buried there." Then Thorwald died, slain by the arrow of the Skraelings.

His men buried him in the place that he thought it well to abide in, and they placed a cross at his head and another at his feet, and they named the place Crossness. They went back to where Leif's huts were, and they put the timber and the mösur wood on the ship, and when the spring had come again they sailed back to Greenland. To Brattahlid they went, and they told Eric of the death of his son, and they brought Leif to his ship, and they showed him the cargo they had brought back from Wineland the Good.

Thorstein, Eric's Third Son

After this it happened that Thorstein, Eric's third son, wanted to make the voyage to the place where his brother was killed, and avenge his death on the people called the Skraelings. He gathered a crew together and he made ready to sail on Leif's ship. Thorstein was newly married then, and he brought Gudrid, his bride, with him on the voyage.

But Thorstein did not have the fair winds that Leif had and that Thorwald had. He and his crew were long tossed upon the ocean, and could not lay the course they wished. They were driven back on their course so that they came in sight of Iceland, and they also saw birds from the Irish coast. They were driven hither and thither over the sea. In the autumn they turned back, worn out by toil and exposure to the elements, and exhausted by their labors. They landed on Greenland, but on the side farthest away from Brattahlid. Thorstein found shelter and lodging there for his crew, and he and his wife stayed two days and two nights upon their ship. Then one who was a namesake of Thorstein, Eric's son, Thorstein the Black, came to them, and took Thorstein and Gudrid, his wife, to live at his house. And there Thorstein, Eric's son, died. Thorstein the Black brought Gudrid back to Brattahlid where Eric the Red still lived with Leif, the discoverer of Wineland the Good.

Gudrid the Fair

Gudrid the Fair dreamt of voyages to the land of woods and grapes and fair pastures. Even the disastrous voyage she had made with her husband did not make her inclined to stay at home—the emptiness and iciness of Greenland did not go with her thoughts.

Often she talked with her father-in-law, that old voyager, about the journeys he had made, across the sea and away from Greenland. And Eric the Red told her of how he had been banished from Norway for the killing of a man, and of how he had gone into Iceland while he was still in his early manhood, of how he had got into a feud with the men of Iceland, and had to flee from that land too. And he told her how he and his friends had gone in search of the land that a man named Gunnbiorn, the son of Ulf the Crow, had sighted but had not landed on, and of how he had found that land and named it Greenland, and had brought folk to settle on it. The old man talked to Gudrid, that fair and wise woman, telling her many things.

Her father had brought Gudrid into Greenland a while before this. He had lived in Iceland and she had been brought up there. Then, because some one he was scornful of had asked for her in marriage, he had sold his land and his possessions in Iceland, to the aston-ishment of all who knew him, for he was blessed with many friends there, and had come over to Greenland to make his home with his friend Eric the Red. And soon after they had come over, Thorstein, Eric's son, married the daughter of his father's friend.

She was named "the Fair," and she was certainly the most beautiful as well as the most spirited woman in Iceland or in Greenland. And now that her husband, Thorstein, was dead, she admired above all other men the father of the voyagers, Eric the Red. He was still a mighty man; he was no longer red in hair and beard, but he was still tall and deep-chested. He was a pagan, and he kept about him men who were pagans and who swore by the red-bearded god, Thor the Hammerer.

Now there came to Greenland a ship that was owned by a man named Karlsefni. Eric the Red came to the ship to trade, and Gudrid, his daughter-in-law, came with him. Those in charge of the ship invited Gudrid to take for herself any of the goods that she fancied, and, after that, Eric invited the master and the crew of the ship to Brattahlid to pass Christmas there.

Goods were brought up from Karlsefni's ship, and the entertainment at Brattahlid was so magnificent that the people said that they could not remember a festival that ever went so finely. And when it was all over Karlsefni went to Eric the Red and asked his permission to woo Gudrid, his daughter-in-law. This permission was given; Gudrid herself was favorable to him, and in a while Karlsefni and Gudrid the Fair were made man and wife.

Spring came on, and then Gudrid began to speak to her husband out of the thoughts that were always in her mind. "We cannot be content to stay here," she said, "where the land is always frozen, and where one sees no trees with fruit and blossom on them. We might go to Iceland where my father lived, but in Iceland there is but little fruitfulness. Why should we not go to that country that Leif discovered and that Thorwald went to—a land of fair pastures and noble woods? You have a ship and Leif would give us his ship; we could go there bringing many more people than went with Leif or with Thorwald."

So Gudrid spoke to her husband. And at the time there was much talk of Wineland the Good, and there were those who said that it should be further explored. Karlsefni listened to his wife, and he listened to what people said about Wineland and about the voyage there. He was an experienced shipman and he had made many ventures on the sea, and the voyage to Wineland the Good seemed to be a thing that he should engage in.

They fitted out ships, and they took cattle and sheep in them, and they got together men and women to the number of one hundred and sixty, and they made ready to voyage to that far land. They brought weapons and they brought cloth. Freydis, Leif's sister, and her husband came, and a man called Thorhall who was Eric's fisherman and huntsman.

They came first to the land that was named for the large flat stones that were on it—Helluland; there they saw many northern foxes. They sailed on for two days more, and turned from the south to the south-east, and came to a land that was covered with woods and that had many wild beasts upon it. This was Markland, named because of its woods. Then they went by strands that they named Wonder Strands because it took them so long to sail by them. They came to where the land was indented with inlets, and they sailed into one of these inlets. There was an island there that had so many birds upon it that it was impossible to step between the eggs they had laid upon the ground. Then they went on shore, bringing their cattle and sheep to land, and taking the cargo off the ships, and there they made a settlement.

They fished in the rivers, but when the fish began to fail they became badly off for provisions. There was distress then, and Karlsefni was blamed for not having made account of what might happen and provided for it beforehand. And Karlsefni was driven to consult with Thorhall the Huntsman about ways of providing for those who were there.

This Thorhall was of giant stature; he was stout and ill-favored, seldom-spoken but often given to abusive language. He was a pagan and he mocked at the religion of his companions. But because of his knowledge of unsettled regions Karlsefni thought that he was a good man to have with them.

He was asked by Karlsefni to help to provide for them. Then Thorhall disappeared. For three days they searched for him and then they came upon him. He was lying out upon a cliff, looking up at the sky, his mouth and his nostrils agape. He was mumbling and muttering things. Karlsefni asked him why he had gone to that place, and what he was doing. He made answer, saying that what he was doing was no concern of theirs. But he went with them, and they all went upon the beach.

And as they came upon the beach Thorhall raised a shout and showed them a whale near by. They went in chase of the whale, and killed it and cut it up for food. While the whole company, men and women, were eating the whale's flesh, Thorhall said to them, "Did not Thor the Red-bearded prove more helpful than the god of the Christians? This whale that you have taken is a reward for the verses I made over there in praise of him. Thor the Trustworthy he is well named; seldom has he failed me when I have made verses for him." When the people heard him say this they ate no more of the whale.

After that the fine weather came; they gathered eggs

on the island, caught fish in the sea, and killed game in the woods. Thereafter they did not want for provisions. They went abroad in the land they had come to, and they saw that it was indeed a fair and a fruitful country, and that their cattle and sheep had good pasturage on it.

Thorhall, after that, with nine other men took a ship and left Karlsefni and his companions. As he went on the ship he sang songs mocking them and the land they had come to. He had been promised wine, he sang, but no wine had come his way.

> *Stooping at the springs I've tasted*
> *All the wine this land can give.*

And as the sail of the ship was hoisted, he sang:

> *Their land let them praise*
> *As their fast they break*
> *On whale-steak.*
> *We'll follow the ways*
> *Of the foam*
> *For home.*

And so, with nine men, Thorhall sailed away. They intended to sail past Wonder Strands, and then make their way around the cape. This they did. But it has been told that as they came near home they encountered westerly gales; they were swept out of their course and driven ashore on Ireland. There Thorhall and his party, as traders have related, were thrown into slavery. And Thorhall, the follower of Thor the Red-bearded, lost his life there.

And now Karlsefni and Gudrid and their companions sailed southward along the coast, seeking the way to Wineland the Good. They came to where a river flowed down into the sea, passing through a lake. There were sand-bars at the mouth of the river so that it could be entered only in the height of the flood-tide. They sailed into the mouth of the river; they took their cattle and sheep off the ships, and they built their huts on that land.

Wild grain grew there; it was in the hollows; on the hills were vines with grapes, Every brook was filled with fish; there were animals to be hunted in the woods. They caught halibut by digging pits on the beach; the tide flowing in left the halibut in the pits. Their cattle and sheep grazed, and the men felt that they need keep no watch. For half a month they remained in that place.

Then one day they saw a great number of canoes

coming across the water. "The Skraelings!" they called out to each other, and they thought of how Thorwald had been killed. The men in the canoes held poles, and they swung them in the direction that the sun moved. "What may these signs betoken?" some one asked. "I think they are signals of peace," Karlsefni said. He had his men take up white shields and display them in token of peace.

Then the Skraelings left their canoes and came ashore. They were ill-favored men, having coarse black hair on their heads, and broad checks. They came on, openly marveling at Karlsefni and his men. They showed skins they had brought with them, and Karlsefni and his people showed the red cloth that they had brought in their cargo, and both peoples began to barter.

For a good skin of a wild beast the Skraelings would take a piece of red stuff a span in length; this they would bind around their heads. They wanted to trade for swords and spears also, but this Karlsefni would not permit.

So many skins were given that Karlsefni and his people became short of red cloth; they began to divide what was left into pieces no more than the width of a finger. These pieces the Skraelings took, giving for them as good skins as they gave before.

The bartering went on for a long time. Then it

happened that a bull belonging to Karlsefni ran towards them, bellowing loudly. The Skraelings were terrified by the rushing, bellowing bull. They dashed off to their canoes, and having got into them they rowed away. And no more was seen of them for some weeks.

The canoes of the Skraelings were seen coming again; this time they were so numerous that it seemed as if a stream was being poured out on the sea. They waved their poles, but this time they waved them in a direction contrary to the going of the sun, and they all uttered loud cries. And knowing that they were hostile to them now Karlsefni ordered his people to display red shields.

The Skraelings sprang out of their canoes. They hurled missiles from their slings. Karlsefni and his people saw them, raise up on a pole a great ball. They flung the ball from the pole; it crashed down, and the sound it made was terrifying. A great fear fell upon Karlsefni and his followers, and they could think of nothing but of fleeing from the Skraelings.

They ran, thinking to make their escape along the river bank, and the Skraelings came after them. As they passed the huts, Freydis, Eric's daughter, came forth. She shouted out, "Why do ye run from such wretches, such stout men as ye are? Ye might slaughter them like cattle. If I had a weapon I should not run from them!" They paid no heed to Freydis, and she went with them,

Freydis took up the sword.

but she went slower than they did. As she went on she found a man lying on the ground; he had been struck with a stone, and his naked sword lay by him. Freydis took up the sword. As the Skraelings came towards her she stripped off her clothes, and she struck the naked part of her body with the flat of the sword. And at this the Skraelings became terrified; they turned and they ran back to their canoes and rowed away.

Thereafter Karlsefni and Gudrid made up their minds to go from that place; the land had many good qualities; was fruitful and pleasant, but their lives there, they thought, would be uneasy, for they would always be harassed by the Skraelings. So they sailed northward and they came to a wooded country that had scarcely an open space. There was a river there that flowed down into the sea. They sailed into the mouth of the river, and lay by its southern bank.

And there they made a new settlement, putting their cattle and sheep to graze there, and hunting in the woods, and fishing in the streams around. In the first autumn that they lived there a son was born to Karlsefni and Gudrid, and they named him Snorri.

They had now come into Wineland the Good, the land that Leif had found, and they did as Leif had done, hewing down timbers and gathering the mösur wood. Their ship sailed back to Greenland with cargo, and came back to Wineland again. But no more people came to live with them there. Then quarrels grew up between the people there, and they divided into parties. The quarrels were between the men who had wives and the men who were single; those who were unmarried would injure those who were married, and take their wives away from them.

Karlsefni and Gudrid the Fair went back to Greenland, taking Snorri, their little son, with them. But they often returned to Wineland and to the town that grew up there, and that was called Norumbega. And when Karlsefni died Gudrid the Fair returned to her own land. Afterwards she went to Rome and she told the chief people there about Wineland the Good and the people whom she and her husband had taken and had settled there. Towards the end of her life Gudrid entered a convent and became an abbess.

Ships from Norway and Iceland and Greenland went often to Norumbega in Wineland the Good. They brought back from it timbers and mösur wood. And then there came to Norway and Iceland and Greenland the plague that was called the Black Death. So many people died in these countries that there were none left to go upon long voyages, and the way to Wineland the Good was forgotten. The people of Norway still speak of the terrible plague that came amongst them then. They speak of it as a hag who went marching through the country with a rake in one hand and a broom in the other. When she came to a valley where there were a few good people she used the rake only, and the good people escaped through the prongs of it. But when she came to a valley where the people were all wicked she used the broom, and she did not leave one to tell of what had happened. Often, it seemed, she used the broom. The voyages and the discoveries that had been made by the children of Eric the Red were forgotten, and if they had not been written in a book there would have been no one left to remember them.

He who told the tale of Eric and the children of Eric then went down from the rostrum. Eagerly then the captains and the wise men whom Prince Henry had brought to the Tower talked over what had been told them, and the night passed.

ON THE TOWER

The night had passed, and, as the dawn came, those who were within the tower went up and out upon the top of it. They saw the sun come up in the east, and lighten the waters of the Western Ocean. Then one who was standing beside the prince repeated the verses of the Roman poet, Seneca—verses that seemed to all of them to be a prophecy:

> *Ventent annis*
> *Secula seris, quibus Oceanus*
> *Vincula rerum laxet, et ingens*
> *Pateat tellus, Tiphisque novos*

Detegat orbes, nec sit Terris
Ultima Thule.

*In the last days there will come an age in which Ocean
shall loosen the bonds of things; a great country will be
discovered; another Tiphis shall make known new worlds,
and Thule shall no longer be the extremity of the earth.*

There was there a young man, a Florentine, who had
deeply studied the writings of Marco Polo, and who had
met and had talked with an ambassador who had come
to Rome from the countries of the East. He stood with
one who was the youngest of Prince Henry's captains.

"There is," said the Florentine, "a short passage to
India and the Islands of Spice, and that passage is a westward one. Let it not create wonder in you that a westerly
region is assigned for the country of spices, which have
always been understood to grow in the East, for those
who sail west will find those lands in the West, and those
who travel east will find the same places in the East. The
islands I have spoken of are inhabited by merchants who
carry on their trade among many nations; their ports
contain a greater number of foreign vessels than in any
other part of the world. The single port of Zaiton sends
forth annually more than a hundred ships laden with
spices. There has come to Rome an ambassador from

these parts; I have been a great deal in his company, and he has given me descriptions of the magnificence of his king, and of the immense rivers in his territory, which contained, as he stated, two hundred cities with marble bridges upon the banks of a single stream. I believe that the distance from Lisbon to the famous city of Quisay, sailing west, is three thousand nine hundred miles. This city is thirty-five leagues in circuit, and its name signifies City of Heaven. Its situation is in the province of Mango near Cathay, and it contains ten large marble bridges built upon immense columns, of singular magnificence. The island of Antilla is on the way to it, sailing west. From the island of Antilla to that of Cipango is a distance of two hundred and twenty-five leagues. This last island possesses such an abundance of precious stones and metals that the temples and royal palaces are covered with plates of gold." The young captain to whom all this was said turned his eyes eagerly upon the sea that the rising sun was brightening. This young captain was to have a daughter; her husband was to be Christopher Columbus.

They all stood upon the top of the tower that overlooked the Atlantic Ocean. More inspiriting than anything the captains had heard or the wise men had spoken of was the sight of the ocean that was spread out before them with the first light of the sun coming upon it. Then from each of those present came the words that were in the chorus that the Roman poet had written—the words that to them standing on the tower and looked over the ocean seemed a prophecy:

Venient annis
Secula seris, quibus Oceanus
Vincula rerum laxet, et ingens
Pateat tellus, Tiphisque novos
Detegat orbes, nec sit Terris
Ultima Thule.

THE GREAT ADMIRAL*

In the last days there will come an age in which Ocean shall loosen the bonds of things; a great country will be discovered; another Tiphis shall make known new worlds, and Thule shall no longer be the extremity of the earth.

This is supposed to be written by Las Casas the Elder to his son, then a youth, and on Columbus's second voyage, when Las Casas accompanied the admiral and was permitted to read the journal that he kept on the first voyage.

---

* See p. 203, "Suggested Reading," for more resources on the pre-Columbian Americas as well as other explorer information.

The Course Westward

No one, my son, may strive to render the elation of the admiral when, coming down to the port of Palos, he saw there the vessels ready for his service. For half the years that he had lived in the world he had striven to gain from the princes of Europe ships and crews and permission to sail in the name of some one of them across the ocean and out into the West. And now the ships were there, and he had permission from the King and Queen of Spain to sail across the ocean and make discoveries in their name and under their protection.

For ten years he had been in the service of the Spanish sovereigns, striving to persuade them and those who were close to them that there were lands in the West across the ocean, and that these were verily the lands beyond India, the lands of spices. And it had happened to him in Spain as it had happened to him in other states that he had been in—there were people to say that he was a madman and one who was bent upon overthrowing the doctrines of the Scripture, and that the king and queen and their advisers should have nothing to do with a man so dangerous. However, the queen listened to what the friends of Columbus told her, and she gave a promise that help would be given him as soon as the wars against the Moors were brought to an end. Then the year 1492 came—a great and a fortunate year. It saw the Christian princes of Spain triumphant over the Moors; it saw their banners borne into the Moorish city of Granada and placed upon the towers of the Alhambra. A great and a fortunate year! And Columbus was there to see the triumph of King Ferdinand and Queen Isabella.

The promise was remembered and Columbus was put in command of the ships; he was made admiral and declared viceroy of all the lands that he might discover; he was even ennobled and became Don Christopher Columbus. And so he left Granada, where the king and queen were having their triumph, and he came to Palos, and he saw there the three ships in which the voyage to the West—the voyage he had dreamed on for more than half his days—was to be made.

I write to you, my son, on the admiral's ship as he makes his second voyage to the West. I write out of what I know of the admiral and out of what I have been permitted to read of his great first voyage. It is wonderful that he has so taken to me, giving me his journals to read, and giving me his confidence about the things that affected him on the first voyage. I say that it is wonderful that he treats me in this way, for he is a man who makes little display of friendliness, and who indeed is rough and overbearing with men, and who has many outbreaks of passionate temper. The great admiral is now about forty-five years of age; his hair and beard have whitened, but a reddish tinge is through the whiteness. He is robust and tall of figure, and has a long visage and ruddy complexion. One has to mark his eyes; they are blue and clear and have an extraordinary keenness; all distances, all mysteries, seem to be pierced by his gaze.

That physician in Florence, Toscanelli, who is now a very old man, had written to the admiral before his first voyage, telling him that the passage westward would bring him to the Indies and the lands of spices. The distance across the ocean, he wrote, is three thousand nine hundred miles. And he told him that by sailing to the west he would come to the famous city of Quisay which is thirty-five leagues in circuit. From the island of Antilla, he wrote, to the island of Cipango is a distance of two hundred and twenty-five leagues, and Cipango, he wrote, possessed such an abundance of precious stones and metals that the temples and royal palaces are covered with plates of gold. The admiral had no doubt but that he would come to those rich lands.

He had been put in command of three ships: the *Santa Maria*, his own ship; the *Pinta*, whose captain was Martin Alonzo Pinzon, and the *Niña*, whose captain was Martin Alonzo's brother, Vicente Yañez. Martin Alonzo Pinzon was a good mariner; the ship he sailed was his own; indeed, were it not that he had brought a ship to the voyage, and had shown enterprise in aiding the admiral's plans, the voyage might not have been made.

On August 3, 1492, the admiral gave the word and the three ships went across the bar, so beginning the most wonderful voyage that was ever made. On the Monday following it was discovered that the rudder of the *Pinta* was loose. Twice it broke loose, and the admiral had to give an order to sail for the Canaries, to have the *Pinta* repaired there, or to find another vessel to take in her stead.

There was no other vessel to be got, and, with much

Such a sight prefigured terrible things beyond.

labor, the *Pinta*'s rudder was repaired; the sails of the vessel were altered, too, so that when she sailed out from the Canaries she was square-rigged. From the harbor of Gomera they sailed on the sixth of September and the empty and untraveled ocean was now before them.

It happened that the peak of Teneriffe was in eruption as they sailed away from the Canaries, and the great bursts of fire and the red glow in the sky at night were very disturbing to the mariners. They had never seen such things before, and it seemed to them that such a sight at the outset of the voyage prefigured more terrible things beyond—whirlpools and flaming winds were what they thought upon. But the admiral was calm and firm, and he was able to give confidence to the crews of the three ships. They were quiet and cheerful for some time after this, but again, when the ships were eleven days out of Gomera, terror came upon the crews. The captains could not understand what had happened nor why the dismay was spreading through the ships, and it seemed as if the terror they were in would make the mariners abandon the voyage. At last the admiral found out what had happened. The pilots when they took the sun's amplitude found that the needles varied to the north-west a whole point of the compass. "We have no other guide but the compass," the mariners cried, "and now we are coming into seas where the compass will be no guide to us. We will never be able to find our way back." The admiral was able to calm them for that day. The next morning the sun's amplitude was taken, and the needles remained true. The admiral then declared to them that the compass could not fail to be a guide to them in these seas, and that the reason he had varied for once was because a star had moved from its place. This statement removed the apprehensions of the crews of the three ships; for the time there was no more talk of turning back, and they continued the voyage westward.

Fortunately the weather in those days was most delightful; the admiral, whose love for nature is beyond any man's I have ever known, wrote in the book that he has shown me that these early mornings at sea wanted for nothing except the song of the nightingales. The weather continued to be fine. The day after he had quieted the crews with his statement about the compass—a statement that was no explanation at all, being given to quiet their terrors—some weeds were discovered near the ships, and upon the weeds a live crab was found. The admiral made much of this creature being alive, telling the crews that crabs did not live far from land. Upon this they became very cheerful, and there was strife amongst the crews as to which vessel would outsail the others and be the first to discover land.

The next day the crews saw a tropic bird upon the sea. "It is known that this bird does not sleep upon the water," the admiral told them, "and it must have flown towards us from some land in the West." Now here, my son, I shall inform you that the crews did not really know the distance the ships had sailed. The admiral had kept two reckonings: one, which was the true one, he kept for himself; the other, which was less than the true one, was given out to the mariners. Thus, on a day when the ships had made sixty leagues, he wrote down forty-eight or forty-five leagues in the log that the crews saw, and on a day when they made twenty-five leagues, he wrote down twenty-two. He did this so that they might not become dismayed at the distance the ships had sailed and were still to sail—a distance that no ships had ever sailed before—and fearful at the thought that they would not have provision enough for the return voyage.

When they were twelve days out those on the *Pinta* informed the admiral that they had seen a great flock of birds to the west. It was thought that these birds were flying towards land. A great mass of dark clouds appeared in the north, and this, too, seemed to be a sign of the nearness of land. The hopes of all the crews were raised by these announcements, and there were some on the ships who thought that they might make land that night. They sailed on upon water so smooth that it might have been the river at Seville; but land did not appear. Then, some days afterwards, pelicans were seen. It was known to all that these birds keep in the neighborhood of land. On another day two or three land birds came on the ship; they were singing; they disappeared next day before sunrise.

But in spite of all those cheering signs the crews began to show by their words and looks that they were becoming uneasy at the length of the voyage, and at the fact that upon these seas they had encountered no wind that might bring them back to Spain. They were fearful now that they might sail on upon these seas until their provisions gave out, until the ships' sails rotted away and their timbers fell apart. Then, on the twenty-second of September, when they were thirteen days out from the Canaries, a head wind came up. This showed the mariners that, at any rate, there was a wind that would carry them back. "This head wind was very necessary, and we must thank God for having sent it," the admiral wrote in the book that he has shown me. But still everything that happened seemed to the crews to be perilous: when the sea was smooth and tranquil, they murmured, saying that there would be never a breeze to bring them back, and when there was a wind that made the sea rise they were also troubled, thinking that they would be wrecked by the rising waves.

When the ships were nearly twenty days out, Martin Alonzo Pinzon, of the *Pinta*, called out from his ship that he was able to see land, and he demanded the reward that was to be given to the one who first sighted land. The crews went into transports of delight. The admiral wrote in his book that he went down upon his knees to return thanks to God for the guidance and help that had been given him. On the *Pinta*, Martin Alonzo and his crew repeated in fervent voices *Gloria in excelsis Deo*. On the *Niña*, the crew clambered up the sails to have sight of the land.

Night fell, and the crews kept talking to each other about the end of the voyage, and telling each other about the land they were coming to. As soon as morning broke they all looked towards the south-west, expecting to sight land; but still no land met their eyes. The ships sailed on. In the afternoon they discovered that what had been taken for land was nothing but banks of clouds.

From the time of this disappointment the restlessness and the fears of the crews grew ever more and more. And now they said openly that the ships might sail this course for months and come to no land; they said, too, that if they kept sailing on for a further length of time they would have no provisions for the voyage back to Spain. The admiral heard what was said, and he was greatly disturbed by it. But he never wavered in his faith that land was ahead of them to the west, and that in a while, if they kept sailing on, the ships would come to it. He would not be influenced by their fears and their murmurs; unless they took his authority from him by force and turned the ships back he would keep sailing on. Instead of letting them see hesitation and wavering upon his part, he had an announcement made to the crews that from henceforth he would take no account of signs of land in the south-west, but would sail straight to the west and the Indies.

The firmness with which he made this announcement and the sureness he showed had an effect upon the crews; something of confidence and of loyalty to him came back to them. This was when the ships were thirty days out from the Canaries.

There was fine weather in these days. "For this I thank God," the admiral wrote in his book; "if the weather had been rough and stormy it would be still more difficult to deal with the crews." Still he kept two reckonings; the one which was less than the true one he showed to the crews so that they might be the less dismayed. But in spite of his cutting off from the true reckoning, the distances became more and more terrifying to the crews—the distances that they were from the land of their homes. There were no signs of land after they had seen the banks of clouds, and the strange, empty seas were terrible to them. There were some who thought that the ocean fell over an abyss that was at the end of the world, and that they were sailing towards that abyss and would go down into it. They became openly rebellious. They demanded of the admiral that he should forthwith turn upon his course and sail back for Spain. A heavier sea than they had met before struck them. Thereupon the crews declared that they had delayed their return too long, and that now they would have stormy seas to face on the return journey. "No more delays," they cried out to the admiral. "Return, return!"

The admiral tried to calm them and to assert his command. He told them how deeply he was possessed by the belief that there was land in the direction in which they were sailing. He told them that this land was the rich Indies. He told them that if they did not reach them, other men at some other time would sail there, and have the honor of being the first men to come upon them from that side of the world and have, likewise, the rich rewards. But now the crews listened to him as they might have listened to a madman. They threatened him. And that they might not take his authority from him then and there by force he promised that if they did not come upon land in three days he would no longer hold them to their course.

*He gave orders to sail in the direction that
the birds were flying.*

At sunrise the *Niña* hoisted a flag at her mast-head. It was a signal that something had been seen from the vessel. But the crews of the other ships beheld the flag without any hope rising within them. Then the Lombard cannon that she carried was fired. This made the crews come together and talk to each other with some eagerness. But although the firing of the cannon was a signal of discovery, no land was to be seen. Then, as the crews looked out, they saw great flocks of birds flying south-west—flying as though they were going to land for their rest. As the admiral watched the birds flying over the empty ocean he wondered if this sight meant salvation for him. Were they flying towards some land near by, or were the flocks of birds migrating from the north, coming from some place thousands of miles away and going to some place thousands of miles away? He did not know what to make of the flying flocks, but he gave orders for the ships to sail south-west in the direction that the birds were flying.

And now there was left him but a few more days. It might be that in a while he would have to return across these seas, and, going before the King and Queen of Spain, lay down the authority that they had given him, admitting to them that he had gained nothing of what he had promised them. Afterwards it might be that some other admiral, better served than he, would sail across these seas and come to the lands that he had sought—the Indies east of the Ganges. But yet he did not despair; in the time given him he would bring the ships to land.

It was then that the crew of the *Pinta* saw canes drifting in the water; they had green leaves upon them, and undoubtedly they came from land to the westward. They picked up a board that seemed to have been carved with a tool. There was another sign: the crew of the *Niña* took out of the water a branch on which there were still rose-berries. These were signs of land that all might believe in, and once again there was hopefulness upon the ships.

On the night of October the eleventh, 1492, as the admiral was standing on the quarter-deck of the *Santa Maria* he saw what seemed to him to be a light in some place ahead of the ship. He called one of the officers to him and asked him if he could see anything; but this officer could see no light from where he stood. To the admiral it was like the light of a wax candle, appearing uncertainly. He has shown me where he has written about this in his book; I am inclined to think that he saw the light, not with his bodily eye, but with his spiritual eye that was illuminated by his faith. None of the others saw any light ahead of the ships.

After the crews had recited the *Salve*, chanting their

evening prayers as is the custom of seamen, the admiral directed them to keep a strict watch. They remained all night upon the decks of the ships, and all were stirred by the certainty that the admiral had imparted to them— the certainty that they would soon look upon the land that was upon the farther side of the Western Ocean.

The *Pinta* had kept ahead of the admiral's ship. A sailor on it sighted the land. All on the ships were filled with exultation, knowing that they were the first men to come to the Indies by way of the Western Ocean.

An island was before them with other islands near by. They saw people upon the island. They had expected to see silk-clad people, but these people were naked. The trees upon the island were very green, and there were many streams of clear water. It was indeed a fair and a fruitful place. And as the ships came towards the island, numbers of the people gathered together, and it seemed that their temper towards the mariners was a friendly one.

A boat was lowered and the admiral went from his ship, his two captains, Martin Alonzo Pinzon and Vicente Yañez, going with him. As he went upon the land the admiral raised up the royal standard of Spain; each of the captains bore a banner with a green cross into which were woven the initials of the names of the King and Queen of Spain. The admiral, after he had

The admiral planted the royal banner of Spain.

taken possession of the island in the name of the sovereigns of Spain, gave presents to all the Indians who were there—strings of beads and other ornaments. And thus, two months after having left Palos in Spain, they came to the first island of the Indies.

The Mask of Gold

Guanahani was the Indian name for the island that the mariners first came to; the admiral named it San Salvador. They came to another island that he named Santa Maria de la Conception, and to another that he named Fernandina. All these islands were delightful for their trees, their clear waters, their bright fruits. About one in especial the admiral has told me, and he has shown me, written in his book, the words that came to him when he was in a place upon it.

He left the ship, and he would suffer no one to come with him to that place. There was there a river, with its water very cool; there was there a delightful meadow with palm trees more lofty than any they had seen before on the islands. Now as he stood there in the fairest of the islands that his faith and courage had brought men to, his tears flowed down. "Behold," he said to himself, "how fair all this prospect is! The peak of Teneriffe is nothing to yonder mountain, either for height or beauty. The fields are as green and as flourishing as the fields in Castile in May or June. The harbor here is so well sheltered that a ship may be held in it by the rottenest of ropes, and the water is so deep that it cannot be fathomed. A most sweet and delightful odor comes from the trees and the flowers, while the melody of the birds is so exquisite that one cannot bring one's self to leave the spot. The flocks of parrots obscure the heavens, and near at hand are a thousand trees with their different fruits.

"And yet I cannot give myself up to delight in any of this beauty. The nightingales sing, but I cannot let myself consider their song. If it were possible to let the sovereigns whom I serve look upon the beauty of the places I have found for them! But this cannot be done. And were I to talk to them with the tongue of an angel about all that is to be seen here, they would say to me at the end, 'Don Christopher Columbus, where are the gold and pearls that you were to bring to us as compensation for the cost we gave ourselves in fitting up ships for your voyage? You have found the Indies, you say. Where have you left the wealth of the Indies?'

"The people whom we have come amongst have little that we can gain from them. They speak of gold that has been brought to them, and of mines of gold, but it may be that we cannot come to the places where the mines are, and the rich kings, in the present voyage.

There is certainly wealth on these islands—aloes and mastic and musk, gums and spices—but I am so ignorant of these things that I do not know how to make use of this wealth."

So he said, speaking to himself in that lovely glade. After a while he raised his head, and walked over to where there was a myrtle tree growing as such trees grow in Castile. "Our Lord," he said, "in whose hands are all things, be my help, and order everything for His service."

There were two Indians there, old men, and they came forward with a present they had brought him. It was a cake of wax. They made signs that where it had come from was a long way off. The admiral was much cheered by the present that was brought him then; he was of the opinion that where wax was to be found there were other and more valuable commodities.

He then walked back to the shore. A turtle had been killed; the shell lay in pieces in the boat, and the ship-boys were purchasing javelins from the Indians who were near at the rate of a handful of shells for a javelin. The Indians were always ready to barter whatever they possessed for what our men chose to give them: had they spices—yea, had they gold and pearls they would have as readily given them as anything else. While he stood there beside the Indians and the ship-boys, word was brought him that Martin Alonzo Pinzon had left the other ships with his ship, the *Pinta*—this without leave from him, the admiral. "He has gone," the admiral cried, "abandoning me without any excuse of necessity or stress of weather, and he has done this out of cupidity—to gain for himself the gold that, as the Indians have signified to us, is on the islands or on the continent west of us." Afterwards it was revealed that a mask, having the nose, tongue, and ears of beaten gold, had been given by one of the chief men of the Indians to Martin Alonzo Pinzon; it was this present that excited his cupidity, making him determined to desert the admiral, and go in his own ship in search of the gold. Doubtless he expected that if he found a great quantity of gold, and was able to bring much of it to the King and Queen of Spain, he would be forgiven his desertion and even preferred above the admiral, Don Christopher Columbus.

The Islands

All the Indians they saw upon the first islands seemed to be young, not above thirty years of age, with fine forms and faces. Some painted themselves with black; others with white, others with red; some of them painted only their faces, while some of them painted the whole of their bodies; others again painted only around their eyes or their nose. Weapons they had none, nor did they seem to be acquainted with the use of weapons, for when the admiral showed them swords they grasped them by the blades, cutting themselves, through their ignorance. They have no iron; their javelins are nothing more than sticks, although some are pointed with fish-bones. And yet the mariners noticed upon their bodies scars as if from wounds.

From the first they showed a friendliness to the mariners. The admiral gave them on his landing red caps for their heads and strings of beads for their necks. Afterwards they came swimming to the ships bringing with them bright-colored parrots and balls of cotton; they exchanged these with the sailors for glass beads and hawks' bells; the hawks' bells, because of their ringing, gave them great delight, and it seemed as if they could never give enough to gain these from the sailors. They quickly learned words and phrases that were spoken to them, and were soon able to repeat them.

They were not the silk-clad dwellers in great cities, the wealthy subjects of great kings, whom the admiral had expected to find on touching the Indies. But it seemed to him that there was a continent near the islands, for when the sailors pointed to the scars upon the bodies of some of the Indians, they made signs that seemed to imply that there were places in the neighborhood from which came people who endeavored to make prisoners of them: they had received their wounds in the attempts they made to defend themselves.

Guanahani is a large and level island, with flourishing trees and streams of clear water; there is in the middle of it a large lake, but it has no mountains. The climate, at the time of the year that the mariners came to it, was like that of Castile in April and May. There are no beasts upon this nor upon the other islands that they came to—no beasts except dogs that do not bark, dumb dogs. There were multitudes of parrots, and in the waters around the islands there are wonderful fishes: some are shaped like dories, of the most delightful hues, blue, yellow, red, and every other color; some are variegated with a thousand different tints. In the sea there are also whales.

Although they were willing to give up all they possessed, it was easy to see that they were a poor and a naked people, and had little but their cotton to make trade with. A few had thin plates of gold hanging from their noses. But no more gold than this was to be seen with the people of the first islands that the mariners came to.

As they came near the island that the admiral named Fernandina, the Indians came towards them in their canoes, bringing them food and water. To each of them the admiral presented glass beads, plates of brass, and thongs of leather, all of which the Indians estimated highly. Here they saw trees that had branches of different sorts upon the same trunk: one tree bore a branch with leaves like those of a cane, and another branch with leaves similar to those of the lentisk. On this island the houses of the Indians were very clean and neat, with beds and coverings of cotton. It was here that they first met Indians with firebrands in their hands, and rolls of herbs in their mouths which they light and smoke. But it seems that all through the islands they have this strange custom. Having lighted one end they draw the smoke by sucking at the other end. The tubes that they use in this way they name *tobacos*.

From the time that the captain of the *Pinta* deserted him, the admiral thought of little else than of obtaining for his sovereigns some testimony to the fact that he had discovered for them, not only the Indies, but the wealth of the Indies. And now, when he would come to a place that was beautiful for its trees and its verdure, he would say, "I have no doubt but that these are trees and herbs which would be of great value in Spain, as dyeing materials, medicine, spicery, and so forth, and I am mortified that I am without knowledge of how to make extracts from them." The most sweet and delightful odors from the trees would put thoughts like these into his mind. And then he would look upon the thin and trifling pieces of gold that the Indians wore as ornaments, and he would say, "I perceive that they are so poor that a little gold appears to them as a great treasure." Sometimes he would say of the beauty of a certain prospect that it was such that he could not tire of viewing it, and then he would sigh, thinking of what he had to search for. He wrote down in his book sentences like these: "How may I tell them how enchanting it is to view the valleys, the streams, the fields of bread-root, the pastures fit for flocks of all descriptions (although these people possess none), the grounds fit for kings' gardens? I cannot bring them even a picture of it all." And I have seen in his book, written with his own hand, these words, "Your highnesses, you may rest assured that these countries are so extensive, so excellent and fertile, that no person is competent to describe them, and, without proof of their own eyesight, no one would believe what was said of them."

The Indians spoke of a place named Samoet, which seemed to be an island or a city, and there, as they signified, there was much gold. The admiral sailed in the direction that they gave him. Once he and some of his men landed upon an island where there were palm trees that bore very large leaves; the Indians used them for coverings for their houses. The admiral went ashore in the boat, and he came upon two houses which he supposed to be fishermen's dwellings. The owners had fled, leaving but a dog in one of the houses, a dog, which, like all the dogs in these places, was unable to bark. Both houses had nets of palm, lines, horn fish-hooks, harpoons of bone, and other implements for fishing. The admiral gave orders that nothing was to be touched in the houses.

The admiral has written about this place in his book. All night, he wrote, they were entertained with the melody of birds and crickets; the air was mild and soft. He heard nightingales, and he says that while the other birds of the place were different from the birds of Spain, there were here the same nightingales. That night as he listened to them he was sure that he would come to Samoet where gold was, and to the great island of Cipango which was described by Marco Polo: it was east of the place that Marco Polo was in, and therefore west of the island that the admiral was on.

He sailed on. Four days later he reached another island, and from what he saw there he came to the conclusion that he was in the neighborhood of the continent. He decided to send an embassy to the king, to establish friendly relations with him, and for envoys he selected Rodrigo de Jerez and Luis de Torres; the last had lived with the Adelantado of Murcia; he knew Hebrew, Chaldaic, and some Arabic; he had formerly been a Jew. To these he added two Indians, one from Guanahani and another from the island he was upon. The envoys were to instruct themselves as to the state of the country;

they were to obtain a knowledge of the territory; they were to observe the ports and rivers with the distances from the places where the ships then lay. He was fully persuaded that within six days they would have reached the continent and would have got back from it.

The envoys returned within the time given them. They informed the admiral that they had reached a town of about fifty houses and of about a thousand inhabitants; every house had a number of people in it, and all were built in the manner of large tents. The Indians, to show their reverence for the admiral's people, kissed their hands and feet, all the time making signs of admiration and wonder. The envoys were feasted with such food as the natives had to offer, while the Indians who accompanied them explained the manner in which their new guests lived and gave a favorable account of their character.

When they left the place the women entered; they, too, kissed the hands and feet of the envoys, and entreated them to remain there. The people did not possess any gold, and the envoys, not hearing of any great towns near, returned to the ships. The admiral then knew that the country of great cities and wealthy kings was not near.

Next he heard of an island that the Indians named Babeque. In that place, the Indians related by signs, the inhabitants were able to collect gold at night by torch-light upon the shore. This gold they hammered into bars. The admiral wrote in his book. "In these places, without doubt, there are vast quantities of gold, for the Indians would not, without cause, give such descriptions—they speak of gold being dug out of the earth and worn in massy ornaments on their necks, ears, legs, and arms. They speak, too, of pearls and precious stones, and of an infinite amount of spices." They told him that in order to reach Babeque he should steer east by south.

Before he sailed the admiral went to view a cape or point of land. About two bow-shots from the cape to the south-east he came upon a stream running down a mountain with loud murmurs. He proceeded towards it, and in the stream he found certain stones which shone with spots of a golden hue. Recollecting that gold was found in the river Tagus near the sea, he thought that the metal might be in this stream, and he ordered a collection of these stones to be made. And while this was being done one of the ship-boys cried out and pointed towards the mountain. The admiral looked in that direction, and what he saw there took his mind (as it seems to me who have read what he has written in his book) from the thought that was now always with him—the thought of the quest for gold.

For growing up the side of the mountain were pine

One of the ship-boys cried out and pointed to the mountain.

trees, the trunks of which were tall and straight to a marvel. "Here," exclaimed the admiral, "is material for the building of the largest ships. Here, too, are oaks, and here is a convenient stream, and a fair site for a saw-mill." And I know, too, what the admiral thought as he wrote this down. He would come here again; he would have ships built here—not three small vessels such as the people of Palos gave him, but great, high, and swift ships. Here he would stay as viceroy of the New World, and he would sail these seas for the length of the continent.

From the pine trees that were here they took timber for a yard and mizzen-mast for the *Niña*. They then went to the bay at the foot of the cape—a bay that was spacious and deep and capable of holding a hundred vessels. A finer port than this, the admiral declared, he could not hope to find again. He wrote that the mountains here were lofty and grandly shaped, and he mentioned the fine streams that ran down their sides. But above everything else he spoke of the pine trees; it gave him inexpressible joy, he said, to behold such timbers before him.

King Guacanagari

The sovereign of one of the islands sent a canoe with one of his principal attendants on board to invite the admiral to his territory. This sovereign was Guacanagari, whose name will be forever bound up with the admiral's in the history of these discoveries. He sent to the admiral, by his principal attendant, a girdle to which was attached a mask, the nose, tongue, and ears of which were of beaten gold.

By this time the mariners had learned enough of the Indian language to be able to communicate with these envoys through the Indians that had remained on the ships since the landing on San Salvador. The admiral dispatched six of his men on an embassy to Guacanagari, and with them he sent his secretary. On their arrival at his town the sovereign took the admiral's secretary by the hand, and led him, accompanied by a great multitude of Indians, to his own house. Food was set before him and before the other envoys, and they were presented with large quantities of cotton cloth and balls of yarn. Guacanagari, personally, gave them three geese and some pieces of gold. On their return to the ships a great number of Indians accompanied the envoys, and they insisted upon carrying their goods for them across rivers and miry places.

The Indians of this place showed more friendliness to the mariners than the people of any other place had shown. On the day that the envoys returned, more than a hundred canoes came to the ships, each canoe filled with people, and every one bringing something as a present—bread, fish, water in earthen pitchers, and a kind of seed which they cast into their liquors and which serves very well as a spice. The admiral mentioned that he would like to have a parrot: immediately this was noised amongst them; they went back and they brought so many parrots that the decks of the two ships were almost covered with them.

It was while the admiral was in Guacanagari's dominions, and before he had yet seen him, that a great disaster befell the mariners. On the night before Christmas, 1492, the admiral, about eleven o'clock, lay down to sleep on board his own ship, the *Santa Maria*. He had had no sleep for two days and nights, and he was quite worn out. The sea was calm; the man who had the helm left his place, bidding a boy take it, and he went off to sleep. This was contrary to the express order of the admiral, who had, all through the voyage, forbidden that the helm should be entrusted to a boy. They were free from any dread of rocks or shoals, for they had already surveyed the whole coast for three leagues beyond that point, and had made sure of a passage for the two ships, the *Santa Maria* and the *Niña*.

All had gone to bed, and the admiral's ship was left in charge of one boy. At midnight the sea was calm—motionless, indeed, as in a cup, but towards Christmas morning the ship got into an unnoted current, and, imperceptibly, was carried towards the shoals. Suddenly the *Santa Maria* struck on them with a noise that might be heard a league off. The boy at the helm, hearing the roaring of the sea, and feeling the current beating on the rudder, shouted out. At that shout the admiral awakened.

He sprang upon the deck before any of the sailors were aware of what had happened—before any of them knew that the *Santa Maria* had run aground. He ordered the men who now appeared to put out the boat and to carry the anchor astern. The boat being put out, the helmsman and many others went into it. Immediately, without waiting for any other order, they rowed off to the *Niña*, which was then about half a league to the windward; but the sailors on the *Niña*, properly enough, refused to take them on board. They sent them back to the wrecked *Santa Maria*, sending at the same time their own boat to the admiral's assistance.

Seeing his own men desert him, and finding his own ship settling down on her side, the admiral was in a state of great trouble. He ordered the mast to be cut away and everything that could be spared to be flung overboard. He hoped that this would lighten her so that she would float again; but the ship continued to settle down on her side. Fortunately the sea had remained smooth. The

Santa Maria began to open between the ribs, and the admiral was forced to go on board the *Niña*.

He had a message sent to Guacanagari, informing him of the great disaster that had befallen. The king dispatched his people to help in the work of saving what was on the ship; with their assistance the decks were cleared in a very short time. On the day after Christmas, at sunrise, the king visited the admiral on board the Niña. No Christian could have been more considerate than he was. He entreated the admiral not to indulge in his grief; he told him that he would give him all his possessions. Already he had given the crew of the Santa Maria the use of two large houses on shore, and he was ready to send as many canoes as might be necessary in order to bring ashore the goods that were saved. The admiral has written down in his book that not even the smallest trifle was taken by the Indians, although they might have taken much in the confusion that followed upon the wreck. "They are honest and free from covetousness," he wrote, "and their king is preeminent in virtue."

The king took the admiral to his own house, and, later, he gave an entertainment for him. On that occasion the king had on a shirt which he had received from the admiral as a present, and a pair of gloves; these last he particularly admired. Conducting him to an arbor that was near his house he presented the admiral to about a thousand of his people. A banquet was served to the king and his principal attendants and to the admiral and the mariners who were with him. The admiral thought that in his manner of taking his food the king showed a neatness that was in keeping with his rank. When he had finished his repast certain herbs were brought him, with which be rubbed his hands; water was then fetched, and he washed them.

When the banquet was finished they went down to the shore. The admiral sent for a Turkish bow and some arrows; these he handed to one of the crew who was expert in their use. The man shot at a mark; this shooting with arrows greatly astonished the king, for neither he nor his people were familiar with weapons. Then the admiral had the cannon fired; the king was filled with fresh wonder, and the Indians were so terrified that they fell down upon the ground.

Afterwards ornaments of gold were brought, and the king placed them upon the admiral's head and neck. These attentions from the king, and the fact that more gold was given him here than on any of the other islands, was an assuagement to the admiral after his great misfortune.

For the loss of the *Santa Maria*, with the desertion of the *Pinta*, meant that he could not hope to sail to the continent beyond the islands, and come to the great city of Quisay where lived the Great Khan. He could not do this, fulfilling the whole of the commission that was given him by the sovereigns of Spain. Nor could he sail to the islands between him and the continent where, without doubt, there was much gold—on one island, he was told, there was as much gold as there was clay. He would now have to sail back to Spain in the *Niña*.

Some of the mariners he would leave behind on this island which he had named Española, and which the natives called Bohio. He ordered a fort to be constructed as quarters for the men he would leave behind. He would have the fort built strongly and have it well manned, not so much as a defense against the Indians, but as a manifestation to them of the mariners' power.

As the fort was being built news was brought to the admiral that the *Pinta* had come to the island and was at the river end. The admiral ordered one of his sailors to proceed to the *Pinta* with instructions from him to Martin Alonzo Pinzon. That evening the king sent him a present of ornaments of gold, begging the admiral to send him in return a wash-basin and ewer; this the admiral did.

The return of Martin Alonzo Pinzon meant that the admiral had now two ships, and with these it would be possible for him to sail to the farther islands; but he was now fully resolved to return to Spain. The captains of

The king placed his own crown upon the head of the admiral.

the *Pinta* and the *Niña*, being brothers, would support each other, and on one of them the admiral could no longer rely. They were ready to overbear him and to cause him trouble of every kind. Therefore, as soon as the fort was set up and manned, he made ready to sail from Bohio. Five chief men of the island, all subjects of Guacanagari, came together to receive him for the last time. They all wore their crowns. Guacanagari led him by the arm to a house. Here was an elevated space, and the king had the admiral seat himself there. He took his own crown off his head and placed it upon the head of the admiral. And in return the admiral took a splendid collar from his neck and put it around Guacanagari's. He also put upon the king's finger a large silver ring which he took off his own finger. The king was greatly pleased with these gifts. Afterwards two of the chief men, kings subject to Guacanagari, each gave to the admiral a large plate of gold.

The king and all who were with him made a great display of sorrow on seeing the admiral go to his ship and on seeing the two ships make ready to depart from the island. And on his part the admiral was deeply grieved at parting from Guacanagari and his people.

He left behind him thirty of his men; they had a strongly-built fort to which they could withdraw; they had in their charge all the goods which had been saved from the wreck of the *Santa Maria*, and which they were to trade with, but to trade with only for gold. He left with them wine and biscuit enough to last them for a year; he left them seed for sowing; amongst the officers he appointed for them were a justice, a ship-carpenter, a caulker, a gunner, an engineer, a cooper, a surgeon, and a tailor—all mariners. He left with the men in the fort the long-boat of the ship so that they might be able to undertake discoveries on the other islands; he wanted them to search for a gold-mine and to mark a favorable site for the building of a city.

Then at sunrise on the fourth of January, 1493, he had the ships weigh anchor. They stood out to sea with a light wind. The admiral took his station upon the *Niña*. Martin Alonzo Pinzon and Vincent Yañez, his brother, still kept up their opposition to him, and this opposition bore heavily on the admiral. The crews were despondent on account of the leaky state that the two vessels were in. Nevertheless, he sailed for Spain with the same fullness of faith as he had in sailing for the Indies. With the help of Our Lord he had accomplished the main object of his quest, which was to have sailed across the empty ocean, and to have shown that there were new lands and new peoples at the other side of it. For, as the admiral wrote in his book, although certain persons have written or spoken of the existence of these islands, they had all rested their assertions upon conjecture. No one heretofore had ever affirmed that he had actually looked upon them, on which account their existence had been regarded as fabulous.

The Voyage Back

On the night of the fourteenth of February the wind increased and a tremendous sea came up. The *Pinta* began to scud, and she was soon lost to sight from the admiral's ship. The cross-sea became more and more terrible, and those on the *Niña* expected every minute to be crushed amongst the waves. The ship was unballasted; their provisions, which had made a ballast, were mostly consumed, and their casks were empty of both wine and water. In that dangerous sea they had to strive to fill the empty casks with sea-water: this they did and a ballast to some extent was made.

The admiral, now feeling a most anxious desire to have his great discovery known, so that the world might be convinced that the assertions made by him had been justified, and that he had accomplished what he had professed himself able to do, devised a method of acquainting the world with the result of his voyage, in case both he and his crew should perish in the storm. He wrote an account of his discovery upon parchment; he had the parchment rolled up in a waxed cloth and well tied; he then placed it within a cask which he threw into the sea. A document that was also within the cask earnestly entreated the finder to carry the parchment to the King and Queen of Spain. None of the crew guessed what was the purport of what the admiral had done; they took it all to be an act of devotion on his part.

At sunrise they sighted land ahead—the first land of Europe. From sunrise until night-fall they continued their course, beating for the land against a violent wind and a heavy sea. They came to the land, but could find no harbor there. An anchor was dropped, but it did not hold, and the *Niña* was obliged to put to sea again, beating to windward all night. At sunrise next day they stood towards the north of the island, and once more cast anchor. The anchor held, and then it was discovered that they had come to the island of Saint Mary, one of the Azores.

On Saturday, February the twenty-third, they sailed out of that harbor, making for the Spanish coast. For most of the night they sailed about seven miles an hour, making sixty miles. Next day there came an eagle upon the ship. It seemed to be the precursor of another storm.

Again there came a wind that drove them from their course, so that the admiral became greatly affected by the thought of meeting such storms so close to their journey's end. A squall struck the vessel, splitting all the sails. After that they had to drive on under bare poles, with a cross-sea and a furious tempest beating upon them. But God was their help, and towards the evening of the next day they saw signs of land; they judged then that they were near to Lisbon.

But still they had to labor against a terrible tempest. The fury of the wind was such that it seemed about to carry the ship up to the skies, and there were violent showers and much lightning. God preserved them until day came, but it was with infinite labor and apprehension on the part of the admiral and the crew.

And when day dawned they found themselves near the rock of Cintra, and near Lisbon. The admiral resolved to enter Lisbon harbor. When the ship was taken within the river the people of the city ran in crowds to see them, wondering at their escape from the terrible sea. They had been offering up prayers all morning for the safety of the ship, for to them it seemed to be in a desperate case.

And so, after that unprecedented voyage, the admiral, Don Christopher Columbus, won back to a port of Europe. He immediately wrote a letter to the King of Portugal, telling him that he had arrived there, after having made a voyage to the Indies by way of the West.

The news of his arrival and of his communication to the king became known, and a vast multitude of the people of Lisbon came down to the ship, to visit him and to look upon the Indians he had brought back with him. They all offered up thanks to Our Lord for the wonderful voyage that had been made in their time, and for the great discoveries that had been made. Then came a letter from the King of Portugal, requesting the admiral to pay a visit to him, and informing him that his stewards would furnish himself and his crew with everything that they stood in need of, free of cost. The admiral left his ship and made the journey to where the king was then staying.

And when he came before him the king caused the admiral to be received with the utmost honor, and he entered into a conversation with him about the voyage and the great discoveries he had made. The queen, too, requested the admiral to make a visit to her; he went and kissed her hands, and told her of the wonders he had looked upon.

On returning to his ship the admiral put out to sea once more, the weather then being fine; he steered south, and before morning the ship stood off Cape Saint Vincent. At noon upon Friday, March the fifteenth, the admiral's ship crossed the bar with a flood-tide and arrived within the port of Palos, out of which they had sailed seven months before.

The people knew the *Niña*; all the bells in the city rang in pride and joy for their return.

Thus Ponce de Leon came to the Fountain of Youth.

THE FOUNTAIN OF YOUTH

When Columbus made his second voyage to the West, Ponce de Leon went with him. To Española he went, and then to the lands beyond. But he came back to Española and was made governor there. And then another land began to fill his thoughts—Bimini.

He built roads and he commanded armies, he raised cities and he meted out justice, Ponce de Leon, Governor of Española. But his thought was upon the land that was three hundred miles away more than upon the land that he governed. Men came to him and told him of Quivera, that city that fronted a river on which floated canoes with prows of gold, great canoes that held as many as forty Indians, each with a crown of gold upon his head. And other men came and talked to him about the lake Guatavita, in which bathed El Dorado, the Gilded Man. He was the king of the Indians there. Every morning at sunrise the priests of his god rubbed him all over with fragrant gums. Then they blew powder of gold upon his body through copper tubes. The powder stayed upon the fragrant gums. All golden that king seemed as he stood upon the raft that, in the sunset, went across the Lake Guatavita. Having come to the middle of the lake the gilded man would plunge into it, and the golden powder that was upon his body would become a gleam in the water. And those who came there with their king would throw into the lake their golden bracelets. The bottom of the lake was laid over with golden dust, and golden ornaments lay upon it. Men came to Ponce de Leon, Governor of Española, and asked help of him to win to Quivera and to the lake Guatavita and to gather the gold that was in these places. But Ponce de Leon thought little upon what they told him, for his thoughts were upon Bimini, the land that is three hundred miles from Española.

There was no gold nor silver there, there were no spices and no pearls. There was a fountain there, and whoever bathed in that fountain or drank of its waters would have again his or her youth, and be as vigorous and as fair to look upon as they had been been the years before they were thirty.

Men had been in Bimini, and they had seen there men and women whom they had known before and in other places. These men and women would not come back to the places that had known them. For they knew that they would be blamed for not living according to the years that they had in the world instead of feasting and making love and dancing under the trees in Bimini. Men had been in Bimini and had seen there those whom they had known as old leaders of armies, old exploring men, old sacristans and old beggars, old maids and old mistresses, and they had come away, scandalized at what they had seen.

A time came when Ponce de Leon gave up his governorship of Española. He gathered the most faithful of his army about him and he said, "We will go to Bimini." He was sixty years old when he said this. He put on the bright breastplate and the polished helmet that he had worn in many wars, he went into all the churches that he had builded, he took farewell of the garden with the orange trees that he had planted and the pool that he had made, and he took farewell of the people, young and old, that he had governed, and he went down to the harbor where his three ships were, all ready for the voyage.

Now there are seven hundred islands in the sea that is around Española, and no one could tell him whether Bimini was or was not on any one of the islands. On every island he went to he heard of searchers for Bimini, white men in great ships and sails, and red men in canoes; they had been there before him and had gone on. Ponce de Leon and his followers drank of the waters and bathed in the waters of every place they came to, and then each man waited to see if the magic change would come over him.

From island to island he went, drinking at the springs and the hidden fountains in each island, and in each leaving behind some man who had given up the quest, and who, marrying an Indian girl, had settled down to live in a straw hut there. Soon there were not men enough left to man his three ships; soon after that there were not men enough to man two ships; then, in one ship, and with but a few followers, he went to the islands in the sea that he had not yet visited.

He came to an island that seemed to have no people upon it. He and his men searched through it, eating the fruits they found, and drinking at every spring and every hidden fountain. The rags that were their clothes dropped from their shrunken bodies. But still Ponce de Leon kept his bright breastplate and his polished helmet. At last on that island they found a human being.

She was an Indian woman: she was stooped and wrinkled, but her voice was yet very loud and clear as she called out to them, "Ye have come to find Bimini; I will go with you and show you the way."

So the crone went down to the ship with them. Ponce de Leon called the island after her, La Vieja, the Old Woman, and he renamed his ship, calling it La Vieja also. She stood at the wheel and she piloted the ship around and between the islands, calling out the names of the islands, and telling Ponce de Leon that Bimini was not to be found on any of them.

She steered for a coast that was south from the islands. The worms that were in that sea bored through the wood of the ship, so that it nearly settled down on the water. Night and day they had to bail the water out. And when they were able to catch a shark and eat it they thought they had a fortunate day. On they sailed, and the seams of the ship opened, and the hoops fell from the casks, and the water they had brought spilled out. But La Vieja still steered it and the ship went on. At last she brought them to a land that Ponce de Leon named. It was Florida; in that land, La Vieja swore, was Bimini, and in it was the Fountain of Youth.

They killed turtles that they found on the shore, and they roasted the meat, and ate, and set out upon the way, cutting through the thickets that were before them.

"I will drink now," said Ponce de Leon.

"To Bimini," Ponce de Leon and his men said—the few men who remained with him—but their voices were no louder than whispers. "To Bimini," La Vieja said, and her voice was loud and clear.

But man after man of Ponce de Leon's followers lay down in the jungle and died. Soon there were none left but La Vieja and Ponce de Leon. They came out of the thickets and went across a grassy country. And now they had companions. For an old horse that had come up to them while they slept hobbled behind them, and an old hound that came out of the grass went limping beside it.

They went towards where they heard birds singing; very loudly the birds sang there, as if every tree was crowded with birds. They went amongst the trees and they went following the heavy parrots that flew before them. And then they came in sight of a glade, and they knew that they were in Bimini, and that before them was the Fountain of Youth.

There were trees there that were the noblest and tallest that Ponce de Leon had ever seen. And the trees stood around a spring, the waters of which bubbled up from the ground. All golden the waters seemed in the light of the rising sun. This was Bimini, but where were the people of Bimini? He called to them, but no voice came back to Ponce de Leon.

As he stood there listening for a voice to come back

to him, La Vieja went down and drank at the fountain. The old horse and the old hound went down and drank. Then the horse and the hound and the Indian woman lay down upon the ground. "I will drink now," said Ponce de Leon, the discoverer of Florida, the Governor of Española. He took off his breastplate and his helmet, and he stooped down to drink at the fountain. And even as he stooped down an arrow flew towards him. It pierced his chest, and Ponce de Leon fell down upon his face, his mouth to the bubbling water. An Indian beside one of the trees had shot the arrow. Now he went and took the breastplate and the helmet that Ponce de Leon had laid down, and he stalked on. The horse and the hound and the old Indian woman lay on the ground, dreaming themselves back to youthfulness.

VIRGINIA *

Captain Barlowe wrote:

O n the twenty-seventh day of April we departed from the west of England with two ships well furnished with men and victuals; on the tenth of May we reached the Canaries, and a month afterwards, on the tenth of June, the islands that are named the West Indies.

Thence we sailed northward, and on the second of July we went into shoal water. Here we smelled so sweet and so strong a perfume as if we had been in the midst

* See p. 203, "Suggested Reading," for more resources on Jamestown, Pocahontas, and the Powhatan tribe.

of some delicate garden abounding with all kinds of odoriferous flowers, by which we knew that the land could not be far distant. Keeping good watch and bearing but slack sail we went on, and two days afterwards we arrived upon the coast. We sailed along the same for about one hundred and twenty English miles without finding any inlet or river issuing into the sea. The first we came to we entered, not without some difficulty, and cast anchor about three musket-shots within the haven's mouth. And after having given thanks to God for our safe arrival we manned the boats and went to view the land adjoining.

Where we first landed was very sandy and low towards the water, but it was so full of grapes that the very beating and surge of the sea flowed over them. After having taken possession of this land in the name of the queen's most excellent majesty, we passed from the seaside to the tops of the hills adjoining; looking from thence we beheld the sea on both sides to the north and to the south, with no end either way. The land we were on stretched towards the west; we found it to be, not a mainland, but an island of twenty miles long, and not above six miles broad. Having discharged our muskets, such a flock of cranes, for the most part white, rose under us with such a cry, redoubled by many echoes, as if an army of men had shouted together.

From the hill whereon we stood we beheld the valleys replenished with goodly cedar trees—they seemed to us to be the highest and reddest cedars in the world, and better than the cedars of Lebanon and the Indies. The island has many woods, and we saw therein trees that bear mastic, and trees that bear black cinnamon, and many other trees of excellent smell and quality. And in the woods are deer, conies, hares, and fowl, and all of these very plentiful.

We were upon the island for the space of two days before we saw any of the natives of the country. Then, on the third day, we espied a small boat or canoe coming towards us, having in it three persons. The boat went to the side of the island; two remained in it, and the third man landed, and walked up and down on the point of land next to us. After we had watched him do this for some time we sent a boat to land; the man waited for us without any sign of fear or doubt.

And after he had spoken of many things not understood by us, we brought him, to his own good liking, on board of our ships, and we gave him a shirt and a hat and some other things, and we gave him to taste of our wine and our meat which he liked very well. Then, having viewed both ships, he departed and went to his canoe again. As soon as he was two bow-shots from the water he fell to fishing, and in less than half an hour he had filled his canoe so that it would just float; he came again to the point of land, and there he divided the fish he had taken into two parts, marking a part for each of the ships, and having made requital for the benefits he had received from us, as much as he might, he departed out of our sight.

And so in friendly wise we came to know the natives of the land which we had named Virginia and which they called Wingandacoa. In a while afterwards they came to trade with us, bringing us deer-skins and bea-ver-skins. The king himself came to us. When we had shown him all our packages of merchandise, the thing that above all pleased him was a bright tin dish. No sooner had he taken, it up than he clapped it before his breast, and after he had made a hole in the brim of it, he hung it around his neck, making signs that it would defend him against the arrows of his enemies. We exchanged one tin dish for twenty skins and a copper kettle for fifty skins; they offered us good exchange for hatchets, axes, and knives; they would have given us anything they possessed for swords, but these we would not let them have on any offer.

The Indians here live in villages far up the rivers; after they had been many times on board our ships they invited us to go to one of their villages. We went twenty miles up a river and on the evening following we came to an island which they call Raonoak, distant from the harbor by which we entered seven leagues.

At the north end of the island there was a village of nine houses built of cedar and fortified round about with sharp fences to keep out enemies; the entrance to it was made like a turnpike and was very artfully contrived. As we came towards it the wife of the king's brother came running out to meet us very cheerfully and friendly.

A feast had been prepared for us, and she brought us into an inner room where she set on the board that was standing the length of the house, venison roasted, fish boiled and roasted, melons raw, and roots and fruits of divers kinds. We were entertained with all love and kindness, and with as much bounty (after their manner) as they could possibly devise. Their vessels are earthen pots made very large, and their dishes are platters made of sweet-smelling wood.

The king brought to visit us his wife and daughter and young children; his wife is a well-favored woman; she wore a long cloak of leather with the furred side next her body; about her forehead she had a band of white coral, and she had strings of pearls hanging from her ears of the bigness of good-sized peas. The rest of the women there had pendants of copper hanging from either ear. The king had upon his head a broad plate of gold or copper—being unpolished we did not know which metal it might be. The men and women are of yellowish color; their hair is black for the most part, and yet we have seen children that had very fine auburn or chestnut hair.

We have now been amongst them and we have seen how they live: they have no edged tools; they make their canoes without ax or other tool of metal. The manner of their making their boats is this: they burn down some great tree, or they take such as are wind-fallen, and putting gum or rosin upon one side of it they put fire into it, and when it is burnt hollow they scoop out the burnt part with their shells. Where they would burn it deeper or wider they lay on gums and burn through them. And by this means they fashion very fine canoes—canoes large enough to transport twenty men. The oars they use are like scoops.

They held our ships in marvelous admiration, and we ourselves and everything we owned were so strange to them that it appeared as if they had never seen the like before. When we discharged our muskets they would tremble for very fear and for the strangeness of it all. The weapons they themselves use are bows and arrows; the arrows are of small canes headed with a sharp shell or the tooth of some great fish, and are sufficient to kill a naked man. Their swords are of wood hardened, and they use a wooden breastplate for defense. These people are loving and faithful, and void of all guile and treason. They care only how to defend themselves in their short winter, and to feed themselves with such meat as the country affords.

Captain John Smith wrote:

We set forward to explore the river some fifty or sixty miles, finding it in some places broad and in some narrow, the country, for the most part, on each side being a high plain, and with many fresh springs. The people treated us kindly, feasting us with strawberries, mulberries, fish, and other provisions of their country: we requited their least favors with bells, pins, needles, beads, which so contented them that they followed us from place to place out of respect for us. Midway in the river we stayed to refresh ourselves on a little island, and there four or five Indians came to us and described to us the course of the river.

There is a place called Powhatan, and the king of the Indians takes his name from that place, and by that name, Powhatan, he is known to all his subjects. We came to where this king was, and he treated us kindly. We went farther on until we reached a place where we were intercepted with great craggy stones in the midst of the river; here the water falls so rudely and with such violence as to make it impossible for any boat to pass; also the river spreads itself out so widely and makes itself so shallow that on either side of the rocks there is scarcely depth enough to float a barge. To the south the ground is a low-lying plain, and to the north there are high mountains, the rocks being of a gravelly kind, interlaced with many veins of glistering spangle.

Not being able to go farther up the river we returned that night to Powhatan; we requited the king's kindness to us by giving him a gown and a hatchet. From thence we went to another place, the name of which I do not remember, where the people showed us the manner of their diving for mussels, in the shells of which they find pearls.

Ralph Hamar wrote:

It chanced that his daughter Pocahontas was her father's (Powhatan's) delight and darling, and it chanced, too, that this Indian maiden had come to exchange her father's commodities for what we had to offer. To the place where she was there came a ship under Captain Argall: Pocahontas would have gone on board the ship to renew acquaintance with certain of the English who were there, but she was fearful that she might be surprised and taken away by our people.

Now Powhatan had taken captive eight men of the

English and he would by no means deliver them up to us; also he had taken with them arms and tools that we were sorely in need of. And when Captain Argall had intelligence of Pocahontas being near at hand and desirous of coming on board his ship he thought that he might redeem some of our English men and their arms by taking her captive; her father, he thought, would ransom her by giving them up.

But how could he get on board his ship this maiden who was so fearful? It chanced that Captain Argall had amongst the Indians one who was his adopted brother; his name was Iapazeus, and he and his wife were friendly with Pocahontas. He went to Iapazeus to have counsel with him as to how and by what means he might make Pocahontas his captive, promising him to use her with all fair and gentle treatment. And he told Iapazeus that now or never was the time to do a service to his adopted brother and to show him the love that he had made such profession of.

Iapazeus, knowing well that his brother would use the Indian maiden courteously, promised to use his best endeavors and secrecy to help him in his design.

Iapazeus then went to his wife, and between the two of them they made a plan to bring Pocahontas on board Captain Argall's ship. And the next day the four of them, Captain Argall and Iapazeus, Pocahontas and

Iapazeus's wife, went down to the water's side. Iapazeus's wife feigned a great longing to go on the ship, and implored her husband to give his permission for her to go aboard. He pretended to be angry with her, telling her that she could not go on the ship without the company of some other women. This denial from him made her weep, seemingly, and then her husband, as if pitying her tears, gave her leave to go on board the ship if it would please Pocahontas to go with her.

Upon this Iapazeus's wife strove to win Pocahontas to go with her. And so earnest were her persuasions that the young maiden at last yielded to them, and forthwith they all went aboard, the two Indian women, and Iapazeus, and Captain Argall. Great cheer was made for them on the ship, and very merrily they went to supper.

Supper being ended, Iapazeus and his wife were given comfortable quarters upon the ship, and Pocahontas was given lodging in the gunner's room. Then they all went to sleep; Pocahontas, nothing mistrusting her reception, slept as well as any of the others did.

Nevertheless, being most possessed of fear and being most desirous of returning, she was first up next morning, and she hastened to Iapazeus to urge him to be off. He spoke to her fairly, but in a while he and his wife got secretly off the ship, leaving her there.

And so in a while Pocahontas came to know' that

she was deserted by those whom she had deemed her friends, and that she was a captive in the hands of Captain Argall and his men. She made no laments and outcries, and if she remained pensive she had yet such dignity as well became the daughter of Powhatan.

Having succeeded in his plan, Captain Argall sent a messenger to her father to tell him that his only daughter was in the hands and possession of the English, and would be held by them until such time as he would ransom her with our men, and with the swords and arms and tools treacherously taken from us. The news was very unwelcome to Powhatan; but he could not without the advice and deliberation of his council do anything of what we asked of him. Nothing was done on his part, and for three months Pocahontas remained in our hands: much was done on our part to persuade her to be patient; she was given courteous usage, and little by little it was wrought upon her that our disposition towards her was of the utmost friendliness.

There was on board the ship a gentleman of approved behavior and honest courage, Master John Rolfe, and he went often to speak with the Indian maiden. And once, speaking with her as the ship was under the shadow of a forest of that land, he saw how noble she was in all her ways, and how she was beautiful with a beauty that belonged to that land. Thereupon he became devotedly hers. And that the time might not pass heavily for her he brought her a bow and arrows and he set up on the ship a mark for her to shoot at. She showed him then how to shoot with the bow as her father's people shot with it. Thereafter Pocahontas and John Rolfe had pastime and merriment together.

Now as to Captain Argall: having succeeded in his design of taking Powhatan's daughter captive and of making himself feared by the Indians, he thought he would use all he had wrought to a greater end than the deliverance of the captive Englishmen with the arms and the tools. He resolved that he would now demand that Powhatan conclude a peace for ever with the English so that the settlement might be without wars and that there might be for ever afterwards friendly commerce and trade between us and the Indians. He increased his force until he had an hundred and fifty men well appointed, and he went up the river towards where Powhatan's chief habitations were, bringing with us Powhatan's daughter, either to move the Indians to fight for her, if their courage and boldness were sufficient, or else to force them to agree to our demands. So we proceeded up the river that was Powhatan's own, and when we came to the narrowest part of it we found there Powhatan with all his men, four hundred of them, all armed with bows and arrows.

Powhatan's two sons were there, and we permitted them to come on board the ship that they might speak with their sister and see how well she had been entertained. Having spoken with her they rejoiced greatly, and they promised that they would do their utmost to persuade their father to redeem her by concluding a firm peace for ever with us. And thereupon Powhatan's two sons left us; they did not return in a certain space of time, and this was a sign for us that Powhatan would not agree to our terms.

And then the young man, John Rolfe, was sent for by Captain Argall and the governor, and he was given orders to go to where Powhatan was and make known to him the English terms. As he left the ship he spoke to the Indian maiden, saying, "It may be that I shall get your father to redeem you out of our hands, so that we shall have you no more upon this ship of ours, and if this befall I shall not be a pleased nor a happy man." Pocahontas made answer to him, saying, "Where you were I was not a captive. I would leave my father's habitation and come back to this ship if you would have me come."

Thereupon John Rolfe went off the ship rejoicing. He rejoiced as he went to where Powhatan and his council were, but yet there was a great anxiety in his heart, for it seemed to him that the terms that he carried meant destruction for Pocahontas's father and his

"Think not upon these harsh terms."

people. He came before them and spoke out the terms that were told him to deliver: they were that Powhatan was to agree to a firm peace for ever between his people and the English, and have his daughter delivered to him, or else to have her sent amongst foreigners. And more than this John Rolfe threatened them with: the English would come back with more ships, and destroy and take away all the corn the Indians had, burn all the houses upon the river, and leave not a fishing-weir standing, nor a canoe floating in the creeks, besides killing all the Indians that they might come upon. But no sooner had John Rolfe given these messages than he said to Pocahontas's father, "Think not upon these harsh terms, but think upon some loving terms that I have in my mind to deliver. I have looked upon your daughter for many days and I love her in my heart. I would marry her if you and our governor would consent to the marriage. And I have a thought that a lasting peace between our peoples might come through this marriage more surely than through any treaty we might make."

Thereupon Powhatan looked upon the young man, and he was pleased with his manly appearance and his straightforward look. He spoke with his council, and in a while he and his council sent for and delivered up to John Rolfe the Englishmen they held captive with their arms and their tools. The Indians had been inclined for war with the English, but now they became more friendly to them and more willing to make a lasting peace with them. And Powhatan also agreed to give Pocahontas in marriage to John Rolfe. And thereupon John Rolfe wrote a letter to the governor, telling him of his love for the Indian maiden and of how his marriage with her might forward a peace between us and Powhatan's people. The governor, being a mild and a gracious man, gave his consent to the marriage. All preparations for war on both sides were abandoned, and the marriage of Pocahontas and John Rolfe was celebrated with all solemnity, the Indians and our people gathering together at the ceremony. Ever since there has been peace between the two peoples, and ever since we have had friendly commerce and trade, not only with Powhatan himself but with all his subjects round about us. And it is truly a delight to see this forest maiden and this young man together as wife and husband. May they and our settlement thrive apace!

THE NAMING OF THE LAND

Fifty years had gone by since the time when the wise men and the captains of his ships had attended Prince Henry in the tower that he had built above the ocean. The tower still stood, and in a room within it there were still maps and charts that Prince Henry had caused to be brought there. Many still came to the Tower to study them.

Into the part of the tower where the maps and charts were, there came two young men; they wore the dresses of traveling students; one was slight and pale, and had a gay manner that went with his blue eyes; the other was fair and blue-eyed, too, but had a heavy head and peering eyes. The name of the first student was Matthias Ringmann, and the second was named Martin Waldseemüller.

"So that you may get on with your great work on cosmography, I have brought you here, friend Martin," cried the first student gaily. "Portugal is the centre of the new world of discovery, you know, and this tower is somewhere at the' beginning of Portuguese discovery. Mark all you see here, friend Martin; these maps and charts and instruments—look well at them."

Martin Waldseemüller did not reply to his companion's remarks. He looked seriously towards where the maps and charts were. And then the two young students saw that there was another in the room, a man who was examining Prince Henry's maps and charts and instruments with great keenness.

He was a man of a very remarkable appearance; about sixty, he was short, with brawny shoulders and arms; his strong neck held up a powerful head; his face was tanned, his eyes wide open and keen, and his nose was long and beaked. And yet for all his powerful appearance and the vigour that went with it, the students could see that the man was kindly and affable; he was richly dressed, and seemed a person who had always had the circumstances of dignity. Now as he went amongst the things that Prince Henry had collected, he examined the charts, the maps, and the instruments as one who well knew their uses.

"Here is a monitor for you," said Matthias Ringmann to his companion. "Draw over to him, friend Martin, and engage him in conversation about one of Prince Henry's charts. He will tell what will help in your cosmography, I will warrant you." Then, leaving his companion standing stock-still, Matthias Ringmann went over to where the stranger was standing, and said to him:

"May I ask, revered sir, if you think that this famous chart of Toscanelli's has need to be revised on account of the discoveries that have been made lately?"

Martin Waldseemüller came close to hear what he would say. The stranger looked at both the young students. And then on Martin Waldseemüller's serious face his glance rested.

"It would be a great gain for me to know what you, revered sir, think," Martin Waldseemüller said.

"Don Christopher Columbus sailed by this chart and came upon a great discovery—the Islands of the Indies," the stranger said. "However, there is a land that Toscanelli had no knowledge of—a land below the Equator."

"That land is indeed a new world," said Martin Waldseemüller eagerly.

"May we ask if you agree with Don Christopher

Columbus that the earth is shaped like a pear?" Matthias Ringmann asked.

"I have reason to think that Don Christopher Columbus may be mistaken in this opinion," the stranger said. "He is a great man and a good man, but the harshness with which he has been treated lately has driven his mind upon self-formed opinions. God grant that his troubles and trials are now over!"

"Does your excellency know Don Christopher Columbus?" Martin Waldseemüller asked.

"He is my friend," he said, "and my son is the friend of his son, that admirable young man, Ferdinand. The fortunes that have been endured by Columbus have wrung my heart. Young men, think of it—think of his sailing back to Española with such high hopes, and finding the fort that he built there destroyed, and the men whom he left behind him massacred by the Indians! Think of his treatment thereafter by judges and soldiers, and that third voyage of his ending by his being sent back to Spain in chains. The admiral of the Indies in chains! The crowds where he landed would not have it so, and commanded the guards to remove the chains from the limbs of the man who had won so much glory for Spain—glory, if nothing else! But Columbus would not have them removed, and he went before his sovereigns with the chains upon him."

"But Ferdinand and Isabella wept when they saw him thus, and they had the chains taken off his limbs," Martin Waldseemüller said fervently.

"They could do no less," said the stranger.

"You have said," said Matthias Ringmann, "that Don Christopher Columbus has been driven back upon self-formed opinions. Would you deign to enlighten us about this matter? We are students, and the young man who has been addressing you, Martin Waldseemüller, knows much about the science of cosmography."

The stranger turned his wide, keen eyes upon Martin Waldseemüller. "Don Christopher Columbus," he said, "has departed from the teaching of the ancients—the teaching that the earth was a sphere. It is a sphere. When he maintains that it is shaped like a pear he is wrong."

"Perhaps," said Matthias Ringmann, "we address one who, as has been the great Columbus, is the maker of maps and charts."

"I have made maps and charts as Columbus and his brother did formerly," said the stranger.

"Perhaps your excellency has been on some of the great voyages that it has been the glory of our age to have undertaken?" said Martin Waldseemüller.

"I have been on such voyages," the stranger said. "I have sailed as a pilot with notable masters. And I have been in charge of ships that sailed to the west, and then thousands of miles to the south, and back across the ocean again to the coast of Africa."

"Oh, how you could enlighten me if you would deign to do so!" Martin Waldseemüller cried. "May I ask if your excellency has written about your voyages?"

"I have written about them, but only privately for friends," he said. "Ah, if I had quiet I should write a book about them, a book that should clear up many mistakes that have come out of what I have written for my friends. If I had quiet, and the help of some learned men, and could reside for a while in my native city, Florence."

Martin Waldseemüller could hardly speak for the excitement that had come upon him. He bowed low to the stranger. "I know now to whom we have the honour of speaking—you are Amerigo Vespucci, the great voyager and discoverer."

The stranger with the powerful head and the wide, keen eyes smiled at the movement of the young student. "I am Amerigo Vespucci," he said.

Matthias Ringmann said, "My friend Martin has talked about nothing else since he read the description of your voyage in that letter of yours that has been translated into Latin by my friend, Father Giocondo."

"Your friend, Father Giocondo, has given me credit

that I did not seek and did not deserve when, in his translation of my letter, he calls it 'A New World.' "

"And the New World has become known through that voyage of yours," cried Martin Waldseemüller, "for whereas Don Christopher Columbus sailed to lands that were already thought of as existing, and whereas Vasco da Gama sailed to the Indies that Marco Polo had gone to overland, you came to lands that the ancients had known only by speculation—to the Antarctic, to the antipodean lands!"

Amerigo Vespucci laughed as he laid his hands upon the shoulders of the young students. "You are young," he said, "and such enthusiasm is becoming in young men. I make no such claims for that voyage."

"But you sailed into seas where our stars are no longer to be seen—where the Pole Star, and the Bear, and the Swan sink out of sight! All that you saw transcended the knowledge of the ancients. Most of them declared that beyond the Equator to the south there were no habitable lands. But you found lands there more thickly peopled than the lands that have been found in Africa. And in the south you saw the bergs of ice and the frozen mists of the north, showing that there is an Antarctic as well as an Arctic land. You sailed into the Antipodes!"

"All that is true," said Amerigo Vespucci. "We sailed south until we came near to an island where blinding snow' alternated with freezing rains. We saw icebergs and ice floes there, and the blood was half frozen in our veins. But it is not of these places I would speak to you, but of other and of fairer places. There was a great inlet that we named 'Rio de Janeiro,' and the land there—I have called it 'The Land of Parrots'—has a temperate and balmy climate, such a climate as I have found nowhere else in the world. The trees grow to such an enormous size there; the shrubs are aromatic, and the birds are of the most brilliant colours. If the terrestrial paradise is to be found anywhere upon this earth, it cannot be far from this region."

"What you have written in your letters is all too scanty," said Martin Waldseemüller. "We beg of you that you write a book about your voyages."

"When I return from the voyage that I am about to go upon, perhaps I shall have quiet enough to write such a book," Amerigo Vespucci said. His eyes went again to the chart he had been looking at, and he began drawing from it, making some rectifications in his drawing.

"The man who saw our stars sink down and new stars appear in the sky," Martin Waldseemüller said, as he looked upon Amerigo Vespucci reverently from the other side of the Tower.

"And what a man!" said Martin Ringmann. "Those shoulders and arms are just the shoulders and arms to guide a ship into the Antarctic seas. Well, friend Martin, you have saluted the discoverer of a new world! Look at him as he leaves the Tower. What a stride the man has! And how magnificently he carries that head with its clear and far-seeing eyes! "

And the two students, Martin Waldseemüller and Matthias Ringmann, watched Amerigo Vespucci leave the Tower and go down the path to the sea.

They sat upon a ledge in the Tower, and one, Martin Waldseemüller, began to think upon the quiet city to which he would go back to give his lectures. If only the great voyager would come there! There he could write his book, and the college of the city had a printing press by means of which many copies could be given to the world. The time was coming when such accounts as Amerigo Vespucci had to give would not be written in a single copy by a man's hand, but would be printed in hundreds of copies. So Martin Waldseemüller thought, his mind moving again to the book on cosmography that he had once, in a burst of enthusiasm, thought of writing, and that his friend, Matthias Ringmann, was constantly urging him to write—an account of the world as it was being revealed by the great voyagers, Columbus, Vincente Yañez Pinzon, Bartholomew Dias,

Vasco da Gama, and Amerigo Vespucci. The quiet city that the students would return to was in Lorraine; it was the city of Saint-Dié, then under the rule of the good Duke René.

"Ours is the city for Amerigo Vespucci to write his book in," said Martin Waldseemüller, speaking after his reverie.

"He will never write it. Such men never write books, friend Martin. But do you note in your cosmography that it is he who is the discoverer of the fourth part of the world."

"I shall note it. I shall give it the name he has given it— 'The Land of Parrots.'"

"What a childish name! No, no, friend Martin, that will not do for a name for the fourth part of the world, I perceive that I shall have to help you in your cosmography to the extent of helping you to great names for great things, Asia, Europe, Africa! These are great names. You will have to find a name as great for the fourth part of the world."

"Santa Cruz, the Land of the Holy Cross!"

"No, no; we want a name that is single and that is grand."

"What name, then, do you think of?"

"Look, I shall write it down."

Martin Waldseemüller looked at what his friend

wrote down. It was "Amerige or America, *i.e.* the land of Americans." As he looked upon it that enthusiasm that often seized upon him came to him there. "It is a great name, friend Martin," he cried, "and I shall use it to designate the fourth part of the world."

And then, in the dust that was upon the ledge of the Tower that Prince Henry built, Martin Waldseemüller wrote the name—

AMERICA

NOTES (1925)

The Tower above the Ocean

"He [Prince Henry] retired to the promontory of Sagres, in the southernmost province of Portugal, the ancient kingdom of Algarve, of which his father now appointed him governor. That lonely and barren rock, protruding into the ocean, had long ago impressed the imagination of Greek and Roman writers; they called it the Sacred Promontory, and supposed it to be the westernmost limits of the habitable earth. There the young prince proceeded to build an astronomical observatory, the first that his country had ever seen, and to gather about him a school of men competent to teach and men eager to learn the mysteries of map-making and the art of navigation." John Fiske, "The Discovery of America," Vol. I. Winwood Reade, too, in his "Martyrdom of Man," gives an impressive account of Prince Henry and the tower he built upon that lonely promontory. Prince Henry was born in 1394 and died in 1463.

Atlantis

The account of Atlantis is given fragmentarily by Plato in two dialogues—the *Timæus* and the *Critias*. The part that makes something of a story is in the *Critias*; in this last dialogue the account ends abruptly.

The Voyage of Maelduin

This story, translated by Dr. Whitley Stokes, was published by him in the *Révue Celtique* for 1888-89. It ends with the words: "Now Aed the Fair, chief sage of Ireland, arranged this story as it standeth here; and he did so for a delight to the mind, and for the folks of Ireland after him." Scholars believe that the tale dates from the ninth century. Whitley Stokes's translation is reproduced in "Myths and Legends of the Celtic Race" by T. W. Rolleston, and there is a version of the story in Joyce's "Old Celtic Romances." Tennyson made a poem about Maelduin's voyage, but he wronged the spirit of the ancient story by putting violent incidents into it. There is no destructiveness in the original; the spirit of the story is shown in Maelduin's speech to the mariner who was hacking at the silver net: "Destroy it not, for what we see is the work of mighty men."

The Voyages of Saint Brendan

The Latin life of Saint Brendan, which was so popular in the Middle Ages, has been combined here with the Irish life given in the Book of Lismore. The most complete account of the Brendan cycle is the Rev. Denis O'Donaghue's "Brendaniana," Dublin, Brown & Nolan, 1895.

The Children of Eric the Red

This is a re-telling of the Saga of Eric the Red and of the history given in the Flatey Book. Scholars think that the Saga of Eric the Red was written down between 1305 and 1334. The following dates should be kept in mind: Greenland, settled by Eric the Red A.D. 986; Leif Ericsson, Vineland, A.D. 1000; Karlsefni and Gudrid, A.D. 1007.

The Great Admiral

"Columbus also made a full report of his voyage in the form of a diary, which he sent to the Spanish sovereigns. The original of this has not been found, but an abridgment, or synopsis, made by Bartolomé de Las Casas, is extant, and has been printed in Navarrete's *Coleccidón*. The transcript of this manuscript, which was probably used by Muñoz and Navarrete, is now in the New York Public Library. An English translation of this 'Personal narrative,' made by Samuel Kettell, was printed in Boston in 1827." Wilberforce Eames's "The Great Admiral" is derived from the translation of Las Casas's abridgment of Columbus's diary.

The Fountain of Youth

The story of Ponce de Leon's search for the Fountain of Youth is one of the first legends that had rise in Europeanized America. Ponce de Leon, who is an historical character, went in search of the legendary fountain. "In 1512 the brave Juan Ponce de Leon, who had come out with Columbus on his second voyage, obtained King Ferdinand's permission to go and conquer Bimini. He sailed with three caravels from Porto Rico in March, 1513, and on the 27th of that month, being Easter Sunday, which in Spanish is called *Pascua Florida*, he came within sight of the coast ever since known as that of Florida. On the 2d of April Ponce de Leon landed a little north of the site of St. Augustine. . ." John Fiske, "The Discovery of America," Vol. II.

Virginia

Captain Barlowe's, Captain John Smith's, and Ralph Hamar's accounts of Virginia are by way of being official reports. There is quite a long interval in time between each of them, but in order to give the sense of a continuous narrative dates have been left out.

The Naming of the Land

"Early in 1507 Waldseemüller had published a small treatise intended as an introduction to a more elaborate work which he was embodying in an edition of Ptolemy.... The book entitled "Cosmographie Introductio" was published at Saint-Dié on 25th April, 1507.... In this rare book occurs the first suggestion of the name of America." John Fiske, "The Discovery of America," Vol. II. Of course the name was not intended to cover what we now know as America, but it was made current, and it was gradually used to cover the two continents of North and South America. Nor was it intended to take any credit from Columbus. His contemporaries and be himself thought that the admiral had reached the shores of Asia by a western route; it was to the south and not to the west that people looked for the discovery of a new world, and Amerigo Vespucci, by sailing into the Antarctic regions south of Brazil, was supposed to have found a world that had no connection with the lands that Columbus had come to. Even Ferdinand, Columbus's son, did not make any protest against the name "America" being written against a part of what we now call the New World.

SUGGESTED READING (2022)

Before Columbus: The Americas of 1491 (Charles C. Mann, 2009). A history of what we now call "the Americas" from the perspective of Indigenous peoples and their thriving societies. Reading age: 8+.

Did Columbus Really Discover America? (Peter and Connie Roop, 2008). Short book covering the historical explorers Colum mentions. Reading age 8+.

The True Story of Pocahontas: The Other Side of History (Dr. Linwood "Little Bear" Custalow and Angela L. Daniel "Silver Star," 2007). This is the first book about Pocahontas, born "Matoaka," which is told by the Mattaponi tribe of the Powhatan nation, as passed down by their ancestors. Reading age: adult.

Pocahontas (Joseph Bruchac, 2005). Bruchac is an author of Native American descent and an expert on Indigenous culture. He consulted the journals of John Smith to compile this book with both Pocahontas's and Smith's perspectives. Reading age: 12+.

SMIDGEN PRESS
Breathing new life into old stories.

Smidgen Press is a boutique publishing house that specializes in classic book republications. We aim to honor heritage texts (and their authors) while restoring old tales to modern bookshelves and e-readers.

Your reviews help other readers find us when you mention Smidgen Press. (Thank you!)

Connect with us:

» Updates, releases, sales: SmidgenPress.com/newsletter
» Suggest a republication: SmidgenPress.com/Requests
» Facebook and Instagram: @SmidgenPress
» Email our team at hello@SmidgenPress.com

Printed in Great Britain
by Amazon

22084869R00124